"So you
or marriage?"

"Oh, no, you see, I have no wish to become a
member of your family.... But I do want
marriage. And since it obviously isn't going
to be you...then I must cut my losses and
look around for someone else."

"Even though it's me you love?"

Roberta lifted her chin to him, green eyes
holding on to his. "And who do you love,
Mac?" she challenged quietly.

MICHELLE REID grew up on the southern edges of the city of Manchester, England—the youngest in a family of five lively children. But now she lives in the beautiful county of Cheshire, with her busy executive husband, and they have two grown-up daughters. She loves reading, the ballet and playing tennis when she gets the chance. She hates cooking, cleaning and despises pressing clothes! Sleep she can do without, and she produces some of her best written work during the early hours of the morning.

Books by Michelle Reid

HARLEQUIN PRESENTS
1140—A QUESTION OF PRIDE
1478—NO WAY TO BEGIN
1533—THE DARK SIDE OF DESIRE
1597—COERCION TO LOVE
1615—HOUSE OF GLASS
1665—LOST IN LOVE
1695—PASSIONATE SCANDAL
1752—PASSION BECOMES YOU

MICHELLE REID

Slave to Love

Harlequin Books

TORONTO • NEW YORK • LONDON
AMSTERDAM • PARIS • SYDNEY • HAMBURG
STOCKHOLM • ATHENS • TOKYO • MILAN
MADRID • WARSAW • BUDAPEST • AUCKLAND

ISBN 0-373-11776-0

SLAVE TO LOVE

First North American Publication 1995.

Copyright © 1995 by Michelle Reid.

This edition published by arrangement with Harlequin Books S.A.

® and TM are trademarks of the publisher. Trademarks indicated with
® are registered in the United States Patent and Trademark Office, the
Canadian Trade Marks Office and in other countries.

Printed in U.S.A.

CHAPTER ONE

'DADDY'S current bimbo...'

In a room stuffed full of warmly alive, happily partying people Roberta Chandler stood alone, battling to stop herself going white with anger around the edges of her red-faced humiliation, while the person who had just used that cuttingly dismissive description of her moved away from the small group of people she had said it to, without needing to glance Roberta's way to know that she had been overheard.

Roberta's heart was pounding, her body trembling with the suppressed desire to retaliate—an urge so strong that she had to force herself to stand very still and stare fixedly at the glass of champagne she was holding to stop herself from doing just that.

Lulu Maclaine would be a much better person if her doting daddy were to wash her nasty mouth out with soap!

What was he? she wondered furiously as the blood continued to pump an angry tattoo inside her burning head. Was he a man at all, or just a pathetic little mouse where his darling Lulu was concerned? Willing to let her behave any way she liked so long as it made her happy?

She glanced up, her glinting green gaze honing directly on to the man who was uppermost in her angry thoughts. He was standing on the other side of the room, talking within a group of people, smiling at some amusing anecdote that one of them was relaying, the

corners of his fiercely sensual mouth curved in lazy
amusement.

Was he totally unaware of the way she was being
treated here tonight? Or just utterly careless of it?
Whichever, he was out of order—right out of order—
and he was very lucky that her manners were so much
better than his daughter's manners, or he would be
tasting a bit of humiliation himself right now!

Damn you, she thought angrily. Damn you to hell for
setting me up for all of this!

Laughter rang out, sounding so wickedly amused that
it drew Roberta's gaze because it represented such complete opposition to her own black feelings just now. It
was Lulu again. Of course it was Lulu, standing in the
middle of another set of guests, holding court in her
lovely blue taffeta gown that was such an exact match
to her lovely cornflower-blue eyes.

'Daddy's bimbo'. Had she just repeated that clever
little remark to her new rapt audience to make them
laugh like that?

Roberta shuddered, feeling sick. She wouldn't put it
past the vicious witch, since she had been saying that or
something like it to anyone who would listen from the
moment Roberta had stepped into the house!

And not only Lulu, she reminded herself. Lulu's
mother had behaved no better, offering Roberta the kind
of cold shoulder all evening that had been a callous
message in itself.

Bitches, both of them. The Maclaine women were
nothing but a pair of lousy bitches.

My God! she railed at herself. Why didn't I listen to
my instincts and stay at home tonight, instead of opening
myself up for this kind of ridicule?

After all, it was Lulu's party. Her eighteenth birthday celebration, to be exact, and perhaps the younger girl had a right to enjoy it without having 'Daddy's current bimbo' present to spoil it for her.

Yet she had been invited! Roberta reminded herself fiercely. Mac had done it himself! And, fool that she was, she'd thought, This time—this time perhaps he means to let them all know how much I mean to him!

What a joke! she mocked herself acidly now. You should have known from the moment he palmed you off on his younger brother Joel for the evening that he was going to pretend that you were barely acquainted rather than lovers. Lovers for almost a year now.

And Joel, she thought suddenly, dragging her angry thoughts over to the other important man in her life—Joel being her boss as well as Mac's brother. Where was he in her hour of need? Chatting up some nubile lady somewhere instead of protecting her from all this flak?

She sparked a hooded glance around the room until she spied him shuffling on the dance-floor with—Lulu's mother, no less.

The two of them were deep in conversation as they slowly circled the floor. Discussing me, probably, Roberta assumed from the expressions on their faces. Joel would be getting ticked off for bringing her here tonight, and he would be using his sandpaper-dry tongue to deflect the scold.

Delia was not pleased. Lulu was not pleased. The whole darned assembly of close friends and relations were not pleased! And why? Because they were all determined to follow nose to tail on the rudeness of their current leader—Lulu. And even 'Daddy' had been very careful to do little more than acknowledge Roberta with one of his benign social smiles so as not to upset his precious daughter!

'Daddy's bimbo'. Not to be offered even the barest courtesy.

Roberta quivered on yet another wave of deep, bubbling enmity, and returned her gaze to where Mac was still standing, looking every bit the powerful leader of men he was in his black dinner-suit and white dress shirt.

Mac. Or Solomon Macmillan Hunter Maclaine, to give him his full and most glorious title. A big, strong name for a man born and bred to take on the world—which he did, very successfully most of the time, running the family engineering empire with a crisp, clear foresight that knocked spots off his nearest rivals. It was only when it came to his private life that things around Mac became decidedly shadowy.

Roberta was one of those shadows, she accepted grimly. His lady of the night, not fit to acknowledge away from the bedroom!

Yet, shadowy or not, angry with him or not, she found that the simple act of letting her gaze rest on him was enough to set those tiny muscles deep inside her body stirring in heated recognition of their sensual master.

And she despised herself for it, wondering why it had to be him. All right, she argued with herself, so he possessed the kind of dark good looks most red-blooded women yearned to know intimately. But she'd met other men of his calibre before without falling flat on her face for them. So why him? Why this man who was, on the outside at least, little different from those other high-powered, good-looking men she'd known and repulsed quite easily?

He moved, half turning in her direction, to listen to something someone was saying to him, and those tiny muscles deep down inside her stirred again in eager anticipation of his noticing her. He didn't, but she got the answer to her question.

Mac stirred her senses like no other man had ever done. It was as simple and as complicated as that.

And it probably had nothing to do with his black-haired, square-chinned solid good looks, but with the inner man, the man she yearned to know, and the one she very rarely got to see, simply because he did not let her—did not let anyone, as far as she could see, except his family, of course.

And Roberta was not and never would be family.

That fact was being patently hammered home to her tonight.

'Daddy's bimbo'. Didn't Lulu see that in calling Roberta that she was also insulting her father?

Look at him! she wanted to yell. Does he look like a man whose tastes in women only stretch as far as empty-headed bimbos?

Who cares if the woman beneath you has a brain or not, a mocking little voice in her head yelled back, when it's not her brain you're taking pleasure in?

And more than half the women present in this room would not want Mac for his dynamic brain either, she tightly mocked that voice. Not if they knew him as intimately as I do!

And it was that intimate knowledge of him that she used now cynically to strip away the conventional veneer of elegance and sophistication that he wore so well around himself, to see right through to the naked beauty of the man beneath.

Tall—he was tall—and superbly constructed with it. A lean, lithe, sleek construction of tight, satin-sheened skin stretched tautly over hard, healthy muscle. Wide-

shouldered with flat, spare hips, and what came in between was so shockingly desirable that it dried up her
mouth just thinking about it. Long limbs, powerfully
built. Good hands with a light, knowing, sensitive touch
that could——

She stopped, sucking in a careful breath of air then
letting it out again slowly. It was best not to think about
those hands, she decided grimly, and fixed her attention
on his face instead. A lean face, with jet-black hair cut
to sweep confidently away from his high, intelligent
brow. His eyes, darkly fringed by thick straight brows
and softly curling lashes, were a most compelling colour
of come-to-bed grey; they drew you towards them like
magnets, urging, promising, lazily admiring——

Another stop. And she forced her attention away from
the eyes to the mouth. A mouth so rawly sensual that
it, too, was dangerous even to look at. Thin but nicely
shaped, it was such an experienced, expressive, unin-
hibited mouth that in intimacy it could be quite ruthless
in its efforts to draw the response it required.

And what was that mouth doing now? she wondered,
once again curbing her thoughts before they went too
far. It was smiling lazily, flashing the odd white-toothed,
devilishly infectious grin now and then, fielding witty
remarks to return them with interest. Like the man
himself, supremely at ease, that quick mind of his ten
seconds faster and sharper than anyone else she knew.

Joel teasingly dubbed him 'Mac the Knife' because of
his sharp wits, but he said it fondly. Joel respected his
brother deeply for the way he had taken on the mantle
of power very young after their father's first serious heart
attack, which had meant Mac's growing up a whole lot
faster than most young men his age would have been
expected to do. Yet he had taken up the challenge with

barely a qualm and, although Joel was no small fry in the family firm, he deferred always to Mac's decree.

Which was why Mac had palmed her off on Joel tonight, of course. He trusted his kid brother to look after his woman for him while he was too busy—or too indifferent—to do it himself!

He happened to glance up and catch her staring at him then, his eyes instantly softening to a warm, smoky grey as he sent her one of those little twists to his mouth meant to be a rueful smile, and tipped his glass at her in acknowledgement. It took all she had in her to return the gesture, though an answering smile she could not manage. She was angry with him and was in no mood to hide the fact. Angry that he could take from her everything she had to offer him, flaunt her unflinchingly around London as his woman yet, when it came to his family, pretend that she meant nothing to him at all!

Just an empty-headed bimbo, too thick to notice how his family saw her as dirt!

Her eyes flashed a sudden bright, menacing green. Mac saw it happen and frowned, a silent question entering his own eyes. Roberta's chin went up, her defiant expression daring him to come over and find out for himself what the look was for!

Impatience flickered across his face, followed by a frowning look of indecision when she continued to stare at him like that, and the desire to come and find out why she was spitting green daggers at him began to war with his determination to keep as far away from her as he possibly could tonight.

Then, with a small shrug of exasperation, he took a half-step towards her, and her senses began to fizz on a bright clamour of triumph when it looked as though she was going to win this particular battle and he was going to come to her!

But, just at that moment, a flash of blood-red silk caught her eye, and she glanced to one side of him just in time to see Delia wind her arm into the bent crook of his. By the time Roberta looked back at Mac his attention had already withdrawn from her, to be centred indulgently on his wife's smilingly upturned face.

Ex-wife, she reminded herself as disappointment sent her racing heart plummeting to her feet. *Ex* damned wife! They had been divorced for almost eight years! Yet to look at them you would think that they couldn't so much as function without the other close by!

God! Jealousy shot like the hot flame of hell right through her, forcing her to lower her eyes, close them tightly, pretend—pretend for her own sake more than anything else—not to have noticed their easy intimacy.

Solomon Maclaine and Delia Curzon had both been just eighteen years old when they were forced to get married because Lulu was on the way. All in all it had been an acceptable match, linking the Maclaine wealth with the Curzon millions, and generally making both families rather pleased at their siblings' misdemeanour. But, from the small amount Mac had told her, the marriage had been anything but idyllic. And the long-overdue divorce which took place ten years later had been inevitable—though not so to their staunchly conservative families or their adored daughter.

Hence the show being put on by both Mac and Delia tonight, and the reason why, as usual, Roberta found herself left out in the cold.

'Had enough yet?'

Starting at the unexpected closeness of Joel's voice, she lifted her face, the nape-length edges of her softly curling pale blonde hair skimming across the expanse of milk-white skin left exposed by the off-the-shoulder design of her black velvet dress as she turned to look into his sardonically smiling face. But she knew that smile; Joel was angry—the little tic working at the side of his jaw told her so. Whatever Delia had said to him had just about finished him off tonight.

So, 'Yes,' she told him. 'I've had enough.' Then, on a sudden burst of grim certainty, she thought, More than enough! and felt a new emotion begin to seethe inside her, one which came from the bitter decay of her own self-respect.

For twelve months she had been playing this game the way Mac wanted it played—being what he wanted her to be when he wanted her to be it. But she was damned if she was going to be marked as 'the other woman' by a load of people she could not care less about just because they refused to accept a divorce that had taken place eight years ago!

Being seen as a man's lover was one thing but being labelled his little bit on the side was very much another!

'Daddy's bimbo'. That telling bit of cruelty was, she realised, having a profound effect on her.

And yes, she decided roundly, she'd had enough. She had honestly and finally had enough! Her relationship with Mac was going nowhere and had no hope of doing so while he considered his family more important to him than she was!

All her life she had played second-best to someone—second-best to her parents, who had been rather shocked to find themselves landed with a baby they had never really wanted. Second-best to their dual careers as wildlife experts, which had sent them wandering all over the world studying the habits of one animal or other while this new animal—a human child—was left behind with whoever would have her so long as their lives were not disrupted in any way. And now there was Mac, forcing her to take second place in his life to a family that was obviously so much more important to him.

And there was the rub, she noted rawly. She was not important enough to Mac for him to care what his attitude did to her. And if the last twelve months had not made him care, then nothing would.

She was fighting for a lost cause, and the realisation of it hit her like a runaway train, smack bang in the chest, lifting her perfectly shaped breasts and dropping them again in a single wrenching gasp of pain.

It was time to cut her losses and get out. Where she loved, Mac only desired. And why she had never realised it before was quite beyond her!

'Uh-oh...' Joel chanted drily. 'Those lovely green eyes of yours tell me that trouble is a-brewing!'

You're not so happy with this situation yourself! she wanted to snap. But, 'I'm quite ready to leave if you are,' was all she replied, holding herself stiffly, forcing her face to reveal as little as possible of what was going on inside her. Joel could see that something momentous was, but then he was standing barely a foot away from her, and also Joel knew her perhaps better than anyone else.

'OK, sweetheart.' Suddenly the mockery had gone from his voice, and he reached out to take one of her hands, squeezing it gently when he felt how much it trembled. 'Let's leave the gracious way, shall we?' he suggested with false lightness. 'Through the door with our chins up.'

'You see too much,' she muttered as he began leading her through the milling throng and out into the empty hallway of Mac's elegant country home.

'And you too little, angel-face,' he replied rather drily, then with a gentle push, which was almost a gesture of sympathy, sent her towards the stairs. 'Go get your coat.'

Her slender body was exquisite in the black velvet, and Joel watched her move gracefully up the stairs. She was beautiful; no one could deny that. Mac would not have given her a second glance if she hadn't been. He liked his women beautiful, blonde, sexy. And Roberta possessed one of the sexiest figures that Joel had ever laid eyes on. She was all soft lines and seductively rounded curves, with skin like milk and hair that bubbled softly around her lovely face. Looking at her, you would be forgiven for mistaking her as the archetypal dumb blonde.

But Roberta Chandler was far from dumb—as those sharply intelligent green eyes would tell you, if you could bring yourself to look that high.

It had been to his advantage that Joel had bothered to look beyond that sizzling sexual allure when she'd come for her interview last year, because it meant that he had got himself the best personal assistant he had ever had, and Mac—by his good fortune of being his brother—had got himself the rarest woman he had ever had.

'Where's Roberta?'

Think of the devil, Joel thought drily as he turned around. 'Fetching her coat,' he replied.

Mac's thick black brows took on a downward swoop. 'So soon? It's only——' he glanced at the solid gold watch that he had strapped to his wrist '—ten-thirty. The night's still young.'

'Is it?' Joel murmured cryptically. 'I thought it well and truly done to death, myself.'

'What's that supposed to mean?' Mac demanded frowningly. 'You've been throwing out sarcasm at me all evening, Joel,' he grunted. 'And I would like to know just what the hell you've been trying to get at!'

'Would you?' Joel just sent him one of his sardonic looks. 'Put a week or so aside some time, and I'll take great pleasure in telling you.'

Mac stiffened, the frown becoming more pronounced. 'What the hell's got into you?' he demanded bewilderedly. 'To listen to you, anyone would think I'd offended you in some way!'

You have, Joel wanted to confirm, but at that moment Roberta appeared at the top of the stairs, with her black velvet evening coat draped across her arm, and Joel lost all Mac's attention when the other man saw her. Those lazy eyes of his darkened dramatically at the enchanting picture she presented as she paused at the top of the stairs when she saw him, then came gliding downwards, eyes cool, face as inscrutable as a face as sensual as hers ever could be.

'What's this?' Mac murmured huskily when she reached them, his expression so tenderly intimate that her senses quivered. 'Running out on me with my kid brother?'

She glanced at Joel, wishing in some ways that it were Joel she was involved with. But, although both men were good-looking, smooth, sophisticated, Joel's wood-ash handsomeness had never attracted her.

'I'm—tired,' she answered Mac quietly, the well-modulated tone of her voice like rich cream on honey, giving nothing away of the cold, hard sense of death she was experiencing inside right now. 'It's been a long day, all told,' she added rather drily.

'The man was in his counting-house, counting out his money,' Joel put in, smiling as always. 'Here, give me your coat.' He took the velvet wrap from her before Mac could grab the honours. 'Take-over deals take it out of one, don't you agree, Mac?'

Mac leaned back against the rich mahogany newel-post, sensing no threat in the way that Joel was smoothing fine velvet over Roberta's shoulders. This was his home and here, where Roberta counted for nothing, he saw Joel as his safe substitute.

'The Brunner deal.' He nodded. 'You clinched it today.' Not a question but a well-informed statement of fact.

'Not quite,' Joel denied, then shifted uncomfortably under Mac's sudden black frown. After all, brother or not, Mac was also his boss. 'But all bar the shouting,' he quickly assured him. 'I fly out to Zurich on Tuesday to tie it all up.'

'Is Franc Brunner playing footsie with you?' Mac asked sharply.

Joel just shrugged. 'He knows he owns the patent to a very lucrative product if placed in the right hands. I can't blame him for being cagey.'

'Well, I can,' Mac argued. 'He approached us, not the other way around. What stopped him signing the deal today?'

'The legal bods his end,' Joel said drily. 'Finding problems when none is there.'

'Deliberately stalling, you mean,' Mac said, and looked grimly thoughtful. 'Do you want me to get involved?' he offered.

'No, I damned well do not!' Joel indignantly replied.
'The Brunner thing isn't your baby, it's mine! So keep
your nose out, big brother!'

'Whoops.' Mac grinned. 'Hit a raw nerve, did I?'

'I can handle it,' Joel said gruffly while Roberta looked
down at her feet, too aware of why Joel was getting so
hot under the collar to want Mac to see it written in her
face.

The trouble with Joel was that he was a hands-on engineer at heart. Show him a revolutionary new product
and he tended to go a bit overboard with enthusiasm
about it. Hence the 'footsie', as Mac had put it, that
Franc Brunner was playing with him. He saw too much
eagerness to possess in Joel's manner and had been
playing on that by pushing Joel for a better deal ever
since.

'Can't we, Roberta?'

His long fingers were stroking the rolled collar of her
coat around her slender throat. But when she didn't immediately answer, they paused to chuck her gently beneath her chin, demanding her support.

She gave it. 'No problem,' she said. 'Nothing daunts
the three musketeers.'

'Three?' Mac quizzed.

'Mitzy,' Joel explained. 'Our indispensable third arm.'
He meant their shared secretary, and Mac nodded in
recognition.

There was no one else wandering around the hallway,
and a short silence fell, broken only by the sound of an
old-fashioned waltz seeping out from the huge drawing-
room to one side of them.

Mac's eyes were on Roberta, moving with a lazy
warmth over her, though he still made no effort to touch
her. 'I'll see you Monday, hmm?' he said. His weekend

was fully booked up here in Berkshire, playing host to the dynasty.

Joel felt Roberta stiffen slightly, the tension in her so fierce it was threatening to snap. She did not reply, and Mac took the answer as read, the lazy look dying away.

'Daddy?' Lulu appeared at the half-open doorway to the drawing-room, her blue eyes narrowing when she saw Roberta. 'Hello, Uncle Joel.' She sent *him* a beatific smile. 'Leaving already? That doesn't say much for my birthday party.'

Joel let go of Roberta to turn and smile at his favourite niece. 'I must be getting old, pug-face,' Joel apologised drily, opening his arms as Lulu glided towards him. 'Can't seem to burn the candle the way I used to.'

'You and Daddy both, then, since he's five years older than you.' She pouted charmingly at both men. 'Perhaps he should take a leaf out of your book and ease up on life a little.'

It was a direct slight at Roberta, but neither by word nor expression did she show how easily the younger girl had cut. Mac was smiling indulgently, watching his daughter exchange fond kisses with his brother, the remark not bothering him.

Except for the shock of jet-black flowing hair, Lulu was more like her red-haired mother than her father—a wand-slim girl with long, graceful limbs and sapphire-blue eyes. She lived with her mother in their St John's Wood home for most of the time, but she adored her handsome father to the point of hero-worship. Mac loved and pandered to this adoration as, Roberta supposed, any doting father would.

But sometimes it was so cloying that it stuck in the throat to watch it.

Like now, as Lulu fluttered her long dark lashes and said, 'Aren't my diamond earrings wonderful, Uncle Joel?' She tilted her head slightly for Joel to get a better look at the exquisite diamond droplets dangling from her ears. 'I think I have the most wonderful daddy in the whole wide world, don't you?'

'Wonderful,' Joel mockingly agreed, observing the simpering sigh and soulful look that Lulu sent her smiling father. Mac had his hands in his jacket pockets, still leaning against the newel-post, looking as he always did—supremely elegant and totally at ease with himself. 'He spoils you, pug-face,' Joel censured teasingly. 'If you'd been my daughter, for your birthday you would have received an envelope with ten quid in it and a letter explaining to you how the magic eighteen means that you go out in the big bad world and make your own way from now on.'

'Oh, you don't mean it.' Flirting outrageously, Lulu pouted at Joel and appealed to her daddy with wide, wounded eyes. Without really having to try very hard she had effectively cut Roberta right out of it all. 'Daddy, tell Joel he mustn't be horrid to me on my birthday!' she demanded.

'Joel, don't be horrid to Lulu on her birthday,' her father obediently complied, laughing through his stern tone. 'Where's that besotted young man you've had hanging on your arm all night?' he then asked curiously.

Again Lulu pouted. 'He's trying it on with Mummy since he was getting nowhere with me,' his daughter pertly replied. 'So if you don't get back in there quick and do something about it, I can see Mummy taking on a toy-boy, and how will that make you look?'

'God forbid!' Mac levered himself away from the newel-post, and Lulu sent Roberta a look of malicious triumph when it looked as though Mac would just walk away without offering Roberta a backward glance.

Then the triumph altered to a glower as Mac paused and turned, his grey gaze colliding with Roberta's green one. 'Sorry you had to leave so soon,' he murmured softly. 'I was about to ask you to dance.'

'Shame, then, that you were too late,' she said, the slight hint of sarcasm in her voice just enough to make his eyes narrow. 'A nice party, Lulu.' She turned that hint of sarcasm on Mac's daughter next. 'Once again, many happy returns, and I hope you get all you deserve in life.'

Joel choked on a cough, and moved quickly as Lulu's eyes took on a decidedly vicious glow. 'Time to go.' He gave his niece another kiss, then moved back to Roberta's side, his smile over-bright as he took a firm grip on her arm. 'Lunch one day, Mac,' he offered as a parting shot, and began pulling Roberta towards the front door where one of the hired help for the evening was waiting to see them out, their car already called for and purring at the bottom of the steps.

The last thing Roberta saw as she swept out of the door was Mac's gaze narrowed thoughtfully on her. He wasn't a fool; he was well aware that her last remark to him had been a reference to the challenge she had thrown out to him with her eyes earlier and which he had decided to refuse.

What he wasn't aware of, she knew, was how much he had left too late.

'That wasn't wise,' Joel said quietly.

'Didn't you know?' Roberta drawled. 'I am not a very wise person.' But I shall learn, she told herself grimly. God help me, I shall learn.

'Get in the car.'

She got in the car and pulled her coat more firmly around her body, feeling cold when really it was quite warm for a September night.

Joel didn't move off right away, but sat tapping the steering-wheel with his fingers while he studied her ruthlessly controlled profile. 'Be careful how you tackle this, Roberta,' he advised after a moment. 'My brother is not known for his good temper when things don't go his way.'

'There is only one way to tackle it,' she said, turning her head slightly away from him so that he wouldn't see the bitterness glowing in her eyes. 'There is an old saying about flogging a dead horse. And, much to Daddy's darling daughter's delight, no doubt, I've decided that I've flogged this one for quite long enough.'

'You've put up with his outrageous behaviour towards you for the last year,' he pointed out. 'So why decide that tonight is the night you've had enough?'

'Put the car in gear, Joel,' she said, refusing to answer—if she had an answer to give him, that was, which she didn't. All she did know was that she'd had enough. And that one small but telling little phrase was going around and around inside her head, until she thought she would go mad listening to it.

'He won't let you get away with it.' Joel moved them smoothly away from the house, the headlights spanning out in a wide arc across the moonless blackness of the Maclaine family's private estate. 'He wants you too much.'

'"Want" being the operative word.'

'He had a hard time of it from the family when he forced that divorce on them,' he reminded her. 'Between them and Lulu he's been made to feel——'

'Start defending him and I'll get out and walk,' she warned.

Joel shook his head, exasperation making him sigh heavily. 'It's a damned long way back to Chelsea from here,' he pointed out. 'And I wasn't defending Mac, just explaining why——'

Roberta's hand went to the door-catch. Joel glanced sharply at her, saw her coldly determined expression and grimaced. 'OK, OK,' he said. 'I'll keep stumm and drive you home.'

'Not home,' she countered, bringing his gaze swinging right back to her. 'Take me to Jenny's instead.'

Joel was silent for a moment, taking in this final piece of information. Then he murmured wearily, 'Oh, God, Roberta, you're just begging for trouble if you keep this up.'

Was she? The way Roberta saw it, she was begging for more trouble by letting things go on the way they already were.

It was strange really, she pondered to herself as Joel drove on in grim silence, but if someone had told her twelve months ago that she would find herself in this kind of situation with a man she would have scoffed in their face! She wasn't the type—had always been determined never to become the type! A life of being shunted from one reluctant relation to another while she was growing up had made her determined that once she had gained her independence she would never make herself vulnerable to another living soul, unless they could prove that they loved and wanted her above everything else in their life.

She'd kept that vow too, right through her college years and on into her first job, accepting dates only with men whose other commitments would mean she was never left waiting for them while something more important held their attention from her. But the trouble with that kind of philosophy was that that type of man usually meant a dead-end man with a dead-end job and a dead-end kind of outlook on life that generally bored her to tears. So her relationships tended to be short and disappointing, never really deepening past the kiss-goodnight-on-the-doorstep stage before she was breaking them off.

Until Mac. When Mac had come into her life, every rule she had stood by had just melted clean away! He was everything she *didn't* want in a man. Busy, powerful, with the kind of business and personal responsibilities that meant he had to juggle constantly with time to make room for her. He'd even cancelled their second date because business had taken him out of the country for a week! She should have backed off then—probably could have backed off if it had been their first date—but, even by then, it had been too late for her. Like the fool she had discovered she was, she had fallen hook, line and sinker for him that quickly. And for the first time in her calm, well-ordered adult life she'd found out what it was like to lose total control of her own destiny. Solomon Maclaine had become her master. She didn't like herself for letting it happen but couldn't seem to do a single thing about it.

He could fill her with a dark and degrading all too familiar disappointment by letting her down at a moment's notice when something more important cropped up. Then, when she was determined that it would be the last time he would do that to her, he would do something wonderful, like turning up unexpectedly with his arms full of flowers and a sincere apology on his lips that would have her heart melting all over again.

But not this time, she told herself grimly. This time Mac had gone too far. And the cold, hard feeling of loss she was experiencing inside told her that no amount of apologising was going to change her mind.

She had had enough.

'Listen.' Joel turned in his seat to look at her as he drew his car to a stop outside the Victorian town-house where Roberta used to share a flat with Jenny before Mac had taken her to live in his luxurious Chelsea apartment. 'Use the weekend to think about what you're going to do,' he advised. 'You're thinking with your emotions right now, but give it a couple of days and you should be using your head again.'

'It's my emotions which are involved with Mac, not my brain,' she drily pointed out. 'And I've been applying common sense and modern social standards to our relationship for a whole year now, and look where it's got me.' Branded, she thought bitterly. Branded a bimbo by a set of people that she wouldn't give the time of day to if they weren't related to Mac! 'It's not me who needs to sort my head out, Joel. It's Mac!'

'He cares deeply for you, Roberta,' he insisted urgently, his mouth twisting when he saw the sudden glint of tears flood her sea-green eyes.

'But not enough,' she whispered, not denying that Mac *did* care for her, in some odd, selfish way. No man could give himself so totally in bed without feeling something for the woman lying beneath him—fleeting though that something was. 'The trouble with Mac is,' she added grimly, 'he wants to eat his cake and keep it. And this cake has gone stale enough to chuck into the rubbish bin.'

'Mac doesn't think you're stale,' Joel protested.

'No.' Her eyes flashed him a hard look. 'But he's taken so many bites out of me, Joel, that there really is very little left for me to offer him!'

Joel sighed—the kind of sigh that said he was giving up trying to convince her otherwise. And Roberta sighed—relieved that he was giving up, because she'd taken just about all she could right now.

'I'll see you Monday,' she murmured, opening the car door.

'And if he calls me up looking for you, what do I tell him?' he asked heavily as she stepped out of the car.

Roberta bent down to look at him. 'Do you really think he will?' she mocked, her mouth twisting bitterly on the answer that Joel didn't even bother saying out loud. 'Goodnight, Joel,' she said wearily, and closed the car door.

CHAPTER TWO

JENNY was surprised to find her old flatmate standing on her doorstep, asking for her old room back. 'OK,' she demanded, once she'd ushered Roberta into the small, chunkily familiar sitting-room and pushed a drink of something strong into her hand, 'what has that selfish rat done to make you refuse the final straw?'

'Not Mac,' Roberta huskily denied, defending him even while she knew that he did not deserve it. 'His family.' And she told her friend the gist of her sudden decision tonight.

'How is it,' Jenny demanded angrily when Roberta had finished, 'that a man of Solomon Maclaine's tough character can be so weak where his family is concerned?'

'He loves them,' Roberta stated simply. 'And feels guilty for letting them all down, so he spends his life walking a fine line between pleasing himself and pleasing them.' Her shrug said just how successfully he managed it most of the time.

'Which gives you the unappetising role of being piggy in the middle.' Jenny grimaced distastefully.

'Gave me,' Roberta corrected. 'I've just resigned from the position, remember?'

'You haven't told him yet,' Jenny wryly pointed out.

'No,' she agreed. 'But I will.'

She had had enough.

'Actually, I feel quite good!' she suddenly announced. 'Beneath the bitterness, of course.' She acknowledged Jenny's mocking look. 'And that's only

27

there because I felt so humiliated tonight. But, other than that, I feel as if someone has lifted a big lead weight from my shoulders. I am no longer Solomon Maclaine's hole-and-corner affair!' she loudly declared. 'Perhaps now I can begin to get some of my self-respect back.'

'He'll be around here looking for you as soon as he finds out you're not at your flat,' Jenny warned.

'His flat,' Roberta corrected, her soft cupid's-bow mouth turning down cynically. 'Mac provided me with that flat because a man of his standing has to maintain certain standards for his illicit affairs!'

'Plus the fact that having me around here cramped his style!'

Roberta couldn't help but smile at that. Built on Amazon proportions, with a full figure and the well-toned muscles of a trained physiotherapist, Jenny could frighten off any man with just a certain look!

'Can I have my old room back?' she begged her now.

'Of course you can!' Instantly Jenny's softer side was gushing all over her. 'Do you think you'll sleep at all?' she asked concernedly as Roberta got up from the chair.

'No,' she admitted. 'But I'll try anyway.'

Surprisingly, she slept quite well. Her head hit the pillow in her old single bed in her old familiar room that possessed none of the luxurious trappings Mac had surrounded her with in his personalised love-nest; his darkly attractive face loomed up into the darkness, wearing that rueful little smile he had offered her before his ex-wife had claimed his attention that evening, and, just as she was conditioning herself for a long night's battle against the weakening effects of that smile, she dropped asleep and dreamed of nothing.

It was wonderful. Like being set free.

*   *   *

'Joel's been on the phone,' Jenny informed her when she walked into the small kitchen the next morning dressed in one of Jenny's tracksuits, a pale blue one with a creamy hood attached to the baggy top. 'He wanted to warn you that, contrary to your opinion, Mac is on the war-path. He's already phoned his place asking where you are.'

Roberta paused on a moment's sharp surprise. So her manner last night had managed to get through to him, or he definitely would not have bothered ringing her.

'Did he tell him?' she asked casually, going to check if the coffee-pot was still hot.

Jenny shrugged. 'He says not. But apparently Mac had been trying your number all night, and he's gone from the puzzled to the worried to the bloody furious. Joel said he was spitting out all kinds of nasty insinuations that Joel found rather flattering since they seemed to team you and him together. But he swears he played it thick and said nothing other than that he dropped you off last night and that was the last he'd seen of you.'

'Good old Joel,' she murmured, thinking, So he's decided to come down on my side, has he? She had wondered. Joel was Mac's brother, after all. 'I could do with a piece of toast,' she remarked. 'I didn't eat a single thing at that lousy party last night.'

Jenny made a sound of impatience. 'He'll be ringing here at any moment,' she cried. 'What are you going to do about it?'

'Me?' Roberta paused as she was about to slip two slices of bread into the toaster. 'I'm going to do nothing,' she said, feeding the bread into the warming slots. 'This is your flat. Your phone. You answer it.'

'In other words, tell him a pack of lies.'

Roberta just shrugged, the strange calmness she had taken into sleep with her the night before still presiding this morning. 'I thought you might rather enjoy the job,' she said.

'Oh, I will,' Jenny murmured with relish. She had a thing about men of Mac's calibre, having been heavily involved with one very like him herself once—with similar heartbreaking results. 'But what if he decides to come barging round here to check?' she wanted to know.

'Come off it, Jenny!' Roberta scoffed. 'You know as well as I do that he daren't leave Berkshire until every last one of his guests has left before him! No,' she said grimly, 'I'm safe until Monday. Which gives me time to clear my things from the flat before I have to face him.'

The toast popped up, and Roberta pampered herself by spreading a thick layer of butter on it before taking it to the table with her coffee.

'You're taking this all very calmly,' Jenny observed. 'I mean, Mac is supposed to be the man you fell head over heels in love with—threw all your high-falutin principles away for. Surely you feel some kind of grief for what you're doing?'

Did she? Roberta bit into her toast while she thought about it. 'Perhaps I'm suffering from shock,' she decided finally, discovering that she was still feeling nothing whatsoever except that ice-cold determination which had come with her sudden decision last night.

The telephone began to ring. Something close to terror hit her spine, sending it jerkingly erect. Not so invulnerable, she acknowledged shakily as Jenny moved reluctantly across the kitchen.

'Shut the door on your way out,' Roberta called after her, calmly enough, and Jenny sent her a bewildered look before doing as she was told.

The moment the door closed, Roberta darted up and switched on the transistor radio. A Saturday morning pop show blared out, drowning out any hope of over-hearing Jenny's side of the conversation through the thin walls separating the kitchen from the sitting-room. She sat down again, shaking all over.

Feeling nothing, my foot! she scoffed at herself. She was a walking grenade with the pin half out.

But determined, she reminded herself grimly. Damned, wretchedly determined.

Jenny came back. 'He seems more concerned about you than angry,' she told her. 'He can't understand why you're not where you're supposed to be.'

'So you suggested he look where?'

Jenny shrugged. 'I reminded him that your parents were home and suggested that you could have gone there. He approved of that idea and rang off to check.'

'Oh, that's all right,' Roberta said after a moment. 'They've already left for warmer climes.'

Gone chasing wild dogs across the Serengeti, having been home only five days to dump off the film of their last field-trip—six weeks studying dolphins in the South China Sea.

Five days. She grimaced. Into their early fifties, and still they barely paused for breath between trips. Still they found no time in their packed schedule to do more than allow their only child a conciliatory phone call to offset any disappointment she might feel for their not having time to meet her, if only for a quick lunch.

They lived in a world of their own, which left no room for unimportant things like daughters. So, what's new? she asked herself as an old bitterness began to boil up inside her. They have a vague idea of what you do for a living, that your birthday is somewhere in the month of October, that you're not short of funds and are in good health. What more could a girl want?

A bit of tender, loving care, she grimly answered her own mockery. A father to hug and lean on once in a while. A mother to run to at times like these, confide her troubles in.

A bit of what Lulu Maclaine had a lot of.

Wow! Blowing the air out of her lungs, she pushed herself up from the table with that bit of revealing envy niggling at her conscience.

Then, No, she told herself firmly. It wasn't just a case of her being envious of what Lulu had that she did not. It was simply that she was not going to take second place to anyone else in her life.

And that, she was determined, was that.

Mac rang the flat half a dozen times during the next two days, and by the time Roberta had come back from her final expedition to the Chelsea flat on Sunday evening poor Jenny was looking flustered.

'He's bloody furious with you, he's so worried!' she said almost accusingly, which wasn't surprising since it was Jenny who had had to deal with his calls all weekend, and Mac could frazzle anyone's nerves when he put his mind to it. 'Don't you think you should put him out of his misery now and speak to him yourself?'

'No,' Roberta stubbornly refused. 'Mac has put me through twelve months of misery. Two short days of the same goes nowhere near paying him back.'

'You went into that relationship with your eyes wide open,' Jenny pointed out.

Yes, thought Roberta on a sigh. Wide open but hopeful. A hope driven by a deep-seated need to be loved and wanted for herself above all others by a man she could love and want above all others herself.

Well, she had found the man she loved and wanted above all others. The only trouble was, he did not love and want her in the same way!

Which, in the end, left her with nothing to be hopeful for.

Roberta was at her desk on Monday morning, dictating to Mitzy, when Mac came through the door like a bullet.

'What the hell do you think you're playing at?' he barked, striding forward to slam an angry fist down hard on the top of the desk.

Mitzy jumped, startled out of her wits by his forceful entrance. Roberta took her time before reacting, but then she had been prepared for this—poor Mitzy had not.

Still, as with a carefully schooled expression she lifted her attention from the stack of papers she had been working on and levelled her cool green eyes on him she had to quell a quiver of alarm. Jenny was right, she acknowledged; he was furious. His grey eyes had turned silver with it; his mouth pulled so tightly across his teeth that he was snarling with it—like a dog. A big, dark and ravaging bloodthirsty dog.

'Do you know the kind of trouble you've put me through this weekend?' he demanded harshly when she didn't reply. 'I've been going out of my mind worrying what could have happened to you!'

'But not enough to bring you rushing back from Berkshire to check if I was all right,' she said, and watched him stiffen up like a board at the thrust.

'What's that supposed to mean?' he growled.

'Nothing.' Removing her gaze from him, she glanced at Mitzy, who was staring directly ahead doing a good impression of a waxwork dummy, and Roberta took pity on her. 'We'll finish this later,' she told the other girl quietly.

'Y-yes, of course...' With a blink and a jerk Mitzy hauled herself out of the chair and squeezed warily past Mac's taut frame to leave the room quickly.

The ensuing silence thumped like a drum—or was it her pulse? Roberta wondered as she forced herself to remain calmly seated behind her desk, looking her usual coolly immaculate self in a slate-grey worsted suit and neat powder-blue blouse, while inside her everything was beginning to burn up on a mad combination of bitter pique and the usual hot, melting breathlessness she suffered whenever she looked at Mac.

Mitzy's timely exit had given Mac time to consider just what Roberta had said, and his eyes had narrowed into harshly assessing slits. The anger in him had damped down to a more manageable level, which meant that he was beginning to realise he had a big problem on his hands with her and was responding accordingly—with his razor-sharp brain instead of his emotions.

'Explain,' he demanded at last. Nothing more, just that one very economical word which none the less said it all.

She studied him for a moment, completely in control of her outer self except for the slight trembling of her hands, which she clenched together tightly on her lap while she decided how best to tackle this.

He too was dressed for business, she noted inconsequentially, in one of his dark, fashionably cut suits that did so much to add to that air of power and success he carried around with him.

She would have felt much softer towards him if he had come barging in here looking like the devil, in creased clothes and with his silky hair mussed by worried fingers.

But he hadn't. Mac might have been concerned about her, but only in as much as he could not understand what was going on. His concern had not stopped him from having a good night's sleep or making himself presentable for work this morning.

Which just went to prove how right she was about his feelings for her, she concluded.

'It's quite simple, Mac,' she therefore informed him levelly. 'I've moved out of your flat——'

'I know that!' he cut in deridingly. 'Having arrived there at some ungodly hour this morning to find it strangely lacking any of your personal possessions!'

'—because,' she went on, as if he hadn't interrupted, holding his slicing gaze with her own supremely calm one, 'I have decided to conclude our relationship.'

He didn't move for the space of several stuttering heartbeats, his stunned eyes fixed on her lovely composed features. Then, 'You've *what*?' he choked, and her stomach turned itself inside out as a strange kind of triumph grabbed hold of her.

She had actually managed to hit him right below the proverbial belt at last!

'You heard me,' she answered smoothly enough. 'It's over between us.' Finished, *finito*, she added to herself cynically. No more.

Mac shook his jet-black head as if he needed to clear it. 'Bunny...' he murmured, the husky sound of his very personal pet name for her wrenching at something very vulnerable inside her. 'What the hell is this?'

Genuine bewilderment had managed to cloud over his anger. His lightly tanned face was suddenly pale with surprise. A tightly clenched fist came out between them, the long, blunt-ended fingers uncurling slowly, as though it took a great effort to make the conciliatory gesture.

'What have I done to bring this on?' he asked.

Done? 'Nothing,' she said. Exactly nothing. And hardened her heart against the appealing picture he made standing there pleading with her like that. He had used this tactic before when she'd been angry with him—and had always won with it. But not this time. 'I have simply decided that it is time to get out, Mac. Surely you above all people can understand that?' It was a pointed dig at the long string of women who had preceded her in and out of his own life.

And he took it, by dropping the open hand, the long fingers clenching up again at the same moment that his mouth clenched also. 'But why?' he demanded. 'And why like this? With no prior warning but just an empty flat for me to walk into!'

Had that hurt? She looked into his hard silver eyes and saw that it had. Mac probably brought the end to a relationship by sending a bunch of roses or a pretty bracelet of diamonds and a thank-you, which meant as little as the relationship itself had meant to him. Did he think that his way was any less hurtful than hers had been?

'The relationship was going nowhere,' she told him, ignoring the latter to answer the former because that deserved an answer; the latter did not.

His eyes narrowed assessingly at that. 'And you—wanted it to go somewhere?' he murmured softly.

Roberta smiled, seeing the trap even as he set it. 'Oh, yes,' she admitted, ever so ruefully. 'I wanted it to.'

'But you knew I wasn't into marriage even before we began.'

'Yes.' Her soft blonde head nodded, then stayed lowered, from where she watched her fingers pleat and unpleat themselves on her lap. Yes, she thought heavily.

She had known, but she had been foolish enough to hope otherwise.

'We agreed to live together, nothing else,' Mac said grimly.

That brought her head shooting back up, green eyes honing on to him. 'But we didn't live together, did we?' she challenged. 'You have your Berkshire home, where I am not welcome. Your Knightsbridge apartment, where I am not welcome. And you have your Chelsea flat, where I am supposed to know my place and keep to it!'

'And when do I ever use the Knightsbridge place?' he demanded furiously. 'Or spend time in Berkshire, come to that?' With a raking flick of his hand he dismissed that argument with the contempt he thought it deserved. 'You know as well as I do,' he went on gruffly, 'that where you are is where I want to be, which knocks that excuse right on its crazy head.'

'Unless you're entertaining, of course.' Despite the warming response she had experienced to his gruff confession about wanting to be where she was, Roberta kept her mind firmly fixed on the point in hand. 'When you suddenly develop amnesia where I am concerned.'

'Good grief!' he gasped, eyes widening as understanding suddenly hit. 'Do you mean to tell me that this is all because of Friday night?' He made a sound that was both impatient and scornful.

'The final straw,' she conceded. 'That's all.'

But he wasn't listening. 'I can't believe it!' he was muttering. 'You're just bloody miffed because I didn't dance attendance on you all night long!'

'You didn't dance attendance at all, the way I remember it.'

'I had other duties to attend to!' he snapped. 'It was Lulu's night. And she, therefore, had first call on my attention!'

'She got it, Mac,' Roberta drily assured. 'She certainly got it! The full, central and undivided attention of most of the room all night—at my damned expense due to your lack of support for me!'

'Lulu said something to upset you?' he asked sharply, really beginning to catch on at last. His eyes darkened, the anger leaving him to be replaced with another look of urgent appeal. 'Listen, Bunny——' he leaned towards her again '—if Lulu—or any of my family—offended you at the party the other night, then I apologise for them. They're all so damned——'

Roberta suddenly shot to her feet. 'They didn't offend me, Mac. You did! You do it every time you pretend I don't exist as far as they are concerned! If once—just once—you had come to my side, forced them to accept me for what I am supposed to be to you, then they would have done—and you know it!' She sucked in a short breath, disgusted with him and herself for putting up with it all for so long. 'Well——' She tried to put a brake on her temper, but it didn't work. Now that it had been let loose it did not want to retreat again. 'I refuse to hide in the cupboard like your guilty skeleton any longer! I have done nothing—*nothing*—to be ashamed of. Yet your family—through you——' she angrily made clear '—has sunk my self-esteem to such a level that it can't sink any lower! And yes——' she nodded tightly '—I've had enough!' The lot, everything she had been bottling up all weekend, was spilling out in one furious wave. 'More than enough! I will not allow myself to be trodden under your rotten family's feet for another day! So you

can take yourself—and your selfish idea of a relationship—and just get out of here!'

'Finished?' he clipped.

'Yes,' she said, and sat down with a bump, drawing
air into her lungs in an effort to control herself. She had
been determined not to lose her temper with him, to
finish this with all the cool aplomb that a man like Mac
would expect from a woman of her supposed sophistication. But that was the trouble, she conceded angrily.
She wasn't really sophisticated at all! She was just a love-
vulnerable fool called Roberta Chandler, forced into
playing an alien role because she couldn't control her
feelings for this man!

And to have him she'd had to play it his way—right
down the damned line!

'So you want out.'

'Not *want*,' she corrected, 'I *have* out.'

'Or marriage,' he derided, shoving himself away from
the desk.

'Oh, no.' She denied that instantly. 'You see, that was
another thing I discovered on Friday night. I discovered
that I have no wish to become a member of your rude
and selfish family. But I do want marriage!' she added
quickly, when he flashed her a look that said he might
be considering throttling her for that particular insult.
'And since it obviously isn't going to be to you——' her
slender shoulders lifted and fell in a shrug '—then I must
cut my losses and look around for someone else.'

'Even though it's me you love?'

Oh, that hurt, and it showed in the way she winced.
But she lifted her chin to him, green eyes holding on to
his. 'And who do you love, Mac?' she challenged quietly.

He swung away, obviously not prepared to answer that
one. 'I learned the wedding lesson the first time around,'

he muttered evasively, going to stand at the window with his hands shoved into his trouser pockets. 'I have no intention of putting myself through that kind of hell again.'

'I can understand that,' Roberta acknowledged fairly. 'But whatever hell your marriage was to you, Mac, you did gain something very precious from it. You gained Lulu, whom you so obviously love and adore—a daughter who loves and adores you in return. Do you think I don't want to experience that kind of bond with a child of my own?' she appealed to the rigid set of his back. 'Do you honestly think that, just because you see your duty to the human race fulfilled in Lulu, I must accept that it can never happen to me because I love you and therefore must concede to your dictum?'

'You're jealous of Lulu!' he swung around to declare.

'I am not jealous of Lulu!' she denied, storming to her feet again as the taunt hit a raw nerve. 'But I am jealous of what you and Lulu have, that I can never have if I don't cut myself free from you!'

'But you're only twenty-five years old, dammit!' he rasped. 'You've got years ahead of you to plan things like home and family!'

She felt herself go icy cold. 'Leave it until you decide that you've had enough of me, do you mean?'

The colour drained from his face, his thickly curling lashes flickering down to hide his eyes from her as he turned back to the window. And Roberta smiled bleakly to herself as her heart flipped over, then lay struggling like a dying fish in her breast. She had just knocked the nail right on top of its indisputable head.

'You've never so much as hinted to me before that you felt like this,' Mac muttered after a long, heavy moment.

'I was waiting for you to show enough interest in my feelings to wonder,' she murmured shakily. 'But you never have, have you?'

Even she heard the contempt in her voice, aimed entirely at herself for her own powers of self-delusion, and Mac's shoulders shifted on a gesture of discomfort as he picked up on it too.

'But that really is not the main issue here.' Grimly she shifted things back on to the right track. 'The issue being that I am no longer willing to have a hole-and-corner affair with a man who can't even acknowledge me for what I am supposed to be to him, in front of those people he cares for, because he is ashamed of me.'

'Now that's a downright bloody lie!' Mac barked, spinning around to lance her with a murderous look. 'You know what you are without my having to spell it out for you!' he bit out angrily. 'You are beautiful, you are bright, you are enchanting to be with, and you're damned fantastic in bed! And any man would be proud to call you his—including me! So stop coming on to me as though I treat you like some dirty secret I keep swept beneath the carpet, because it just isn't true!'

'Isn't it?'

'No, it bloody well isn't,' he growled, advancing on her with wrathful intent gleaming in his eyes. 'You are the first woman in ten years that I've given my complete loyalty to!' he reminded her as he reached her.

'But I gave you a whole lot more than that.' She had been referring to her love but, typical Mac, he completely misunderstood her.

'Yes!' he hissed. 'And I have never ceased to be grateful for the honour of being your first lover!' he mocked her cuttingly. 'But if you think I am going to pay for it by being cornered into marrying you, then you have another think coming!'

'But I told you,' she reminded him, 'I don't want to marry you.'

'Then what the hell do you want?' he shouted.

'Out,' she said simply. 'I just want out.'

'God in heaven, woman—no!' he rasped, and reached for her, his fingers digging into her shoulders as he tugged her up against him. 'No,' he repeated, and brought his mouth down hard upon her own.

She had been doing fine until then, Roberta thought wretchedly as Mac began a ruthless plundering of her mouth. She had been managing to hold all these traitorous feelings right at bay—until he'd touched her. And now—now...

She groaned, trying desperately to pull away from him before her clamouring senses got the better of her. But he was big and strong and hungry, and the angry aggression in him answered a softer feminine need inside her to be mastered by his superior will. Her lips parted to the demanding pressure of his mouth without his having to try hard to make it, and on the sensual caress of his tongue she yielded—yielded like a weak little kitten to the superior dominance of the big, powerful cat.

'If I'd been here,' he muttered against her clinging mouth, 'you wouldn't have got as far as packing your damned lipstick!' He moved his hands in a possessive gesture down her body. 'We would have been doing this in two seconds flat instead, and any talk of leaving me would have flown right out of the nearest window!'

She couldn't deny it. Her senses were on fire already. He was angry, which only heightened her awareness of him. And he was a little frightened; she could tell by the tremor in his fingers as they moved over her, by the way his voice had deepened into thick huskiness as he spoke, all of which touched that softer part of her that she had tried so hard to lock away.

He kissed her deeply, his body straining against her, moving with a hot and hungry need that made her own flesh burn, her senses throb and the breath leave her lungs on low, anguished little sobs while she tried so hard to fight her own feelings as much as his heated seduction.

But to no avail. And it was Mac who brought it all to an end, pushing her to arm's length then holding her there while he studied her through hard, narrowed eyes, his own breathing no steadier than her own as she stood there swaying dizzily.

'Where did you go this weekend?' he demanded.

'Jenny's,' she answered, having to fight not to fling herself back into his arms.

'Bitch!' he rasped. 'Did Joel take you there?'

'I...' She lifted a trembling hand to push her hair away from her face, still too dazed to think clearly. 'I w-went after he dropped me off,' she lied, but the hesitation had damned her, and Joel too.

Mac's face turned to granite. 'That's brotherly loyalty for you!' he muttered tightly.

'What he did he did for me!' Roberta insisted. 'That doesn't make him disloyal to you.'

'It doesn't?' he jeered. 'In my book it makes him a bloody traitor!' Grabbing hold of her chin, he lifted it threateningly. 'Where else has he been deceiving me, I wonder?' he grated. 'With you, perhaps? Has my kid brother been trying his luck with you, Roberta? Is that what this is really all about?'

Angrily she pulled away from him. 'That is a disgraceful thing to suggest!'

'No more disgraceful than the insults you've been throwing at me since I came in here,' he defended. 'Joel fancies you. He always has, and don't try telling me otherwise.'

'You're crazy if you believe that,' she sighed, shakily trying to pull herself together.

'Not crazy,' he denied. 'Just aware of what's going on around me. Joel always did want you for himself, and the only reason he has never made a serious move on you before is because I threatened to knock his block off if he ever did.'

'Then why throw us together the other night, if you really believe that?' Roberta cried in angry amazement.

'Because I thought his respect for me meant more to him than his desire for you,' Mac stated. 'But I'm beginning to see that I was wrong.'

'Wrong about a lot of things, if you honestly believe either Joel or myself would do such an underhand thing as to play you false!' Roberta cried.

'Whatever.' Mac just shrugged all of that aside, his attention suddenly fixed on the gold watch gleaming at his wrist. 'I'll be putting him straight before too long.' Grimly he turned and strode towards the door. 'I'll come down and collect you after work,' he informed her curtly. 'Then we'll go to Jenny's together to move your things back to Chelsea.'

'I'm not coming back to you, Mac,' she told him, looking pale but adamant.

He turned to lance her with a look, the contempt she read in his eyes totally new to her and hurtful. 'Do I have to come back there and repeat the lesson?' he demanded, putting shamed colour into her cheeks as he flicked his eyes insolently over the way she was still standing there, shaking in the aftermath of his last assault. 'I could take you here and now on this floor if I wanted to, and you know it,' he jeered, 'so stop trying to draw things out. You've made your protest and it has been duly noted. Now we return to the status quo.'

'No!' she protested. 'Mac——'

'Six o'clock,' he clipped out, arrogantly cutting across any protest she had been about to make before he slammed out of the room.

Roberta stood staring at the closed door, bubbling with anger and frustration, wondering just how he had managed to turn the whole thing round to suit himself like that.

Easy, a small voice taunted in her head. You made it easy for him by falling so easily into his arms!

'Damn,' she exploded softly, then heard another door beyond her own slam shut, and cursed again.

Joel's office door. True to his word, Mac had gone to take the rest of his anger out on Joel. Guiltily aware that she had well and truly dropped Joel in it with her stupid tongue, she dropped heavily back into her chair, wondering grimly if she would still have a job by the end of this horrible morning.

CHAPTER THREE

JOEL was waiting for him when Mac strode into his office.

'Loyal brother you are,' he barked.

'Loyal lover are you,' Joel returned the insult. 'I wouldn't subject my worst enemy to what you subjected Roberta to on Friday night, and that's the truth,' he said, then lazed back in his chair to watch curiously as two strips of guilty colour washed across Mac's high cheekbones.

'Roberta can fight her own battles without your needing to play the shining knight!' he muttered.

'Turned my PA to pulp, have we?' Joel mocked that argument. Roberta could no more fight Mac and win than she could win against a head-on collision with a double-decker bus. 'So now you thought you'd try pulverising me. Well, sorry, big brother, but I refuse to play. You're a fool, if you want to hear the truth—which I don't for one minute think you do. Roberta is one in a million, and you've let her slip right through your selfish fingers because you care more for keeping the damned peace on the home front than you care for her.'

'Don't sermonise over me,' Mac grated. 'Not after the way you've played me for a fool all weekend. How many times did I call you up?'

'Oh, about ten,' Joel answered carelessly. 'Pity you didn't stop phoning and start driving, isn't it? You might just have caught her between moves then. Ah...' he breathed as Mac stiffened. 'So Roberta pointed out the same error, did she? You've got to give it to that girl——' he smiled '—she's honest to the last full-stop.'

'I had other commitments this weekend,' Mac defended himself gruffly. 'She knew that, and if she cared she would have understood.'

'Like you understood how humiliating it was for her to be palmed off on your kid brother at your daughter's birthday party?'

'Oh, go to hell, Joel,' Mac sighed, running a hand around the back of his neck then throwing himself into a chair. 'You know how sensitive Lulu is about me and her mother. It was her night; I had to put her feelings first.'

'Then why invite Roberta at all?'

'Why did she have to accept?' Mac shot back, and Joel sucked in a short breath, the handsome lines of his face hardening as he stared at his brother.

'You bastard,' he breathed. 'You were covering yourself! Playing a let's-keep-everyone-happy game so that Solomon Maclaine could feel comfortable with his conscience! My God,' he muttered as he threw himself forward in his chair and glared at Mac, 'you really are a selfish swine, aren't you?'

'You knew the score when you agreed to take her as your partner,' Mac derided Joel's derision.

'I did that for Roberta's sake, not yours,' he made acidly clear. 'I warned her not to go. I said it wasn't worth the pain our lot would put her through. But do you know what she said?' he offered tightly. 'She said, "This time, Joel, he'll show them. If he cares for me at all, he'll show them." God——!' He threw himself back in his chair, heaving in an unsteady breath of air as Mac squirmed a little. 'No chance, poor kid!' he sighed. 'While she looks at you with hope in her eyes all you

see is what a good lay she is in bed! And that just about
says it all, doesn't it, Mac?' he concluded harshly.

'You wouldn't say no to her if she was available,' Mac
jeered, coming back fighting because Joel had hit more
than a couple of very raw spots in his conscience.

Joel eyed him curiously. 'But she is available now, isn't
she?'

'Taken a fancy to my leavings, Joel?' Mac threw back
nastily.

'Why not?' Joel countered, a strange, whimsical look
crossing his face. 'We've shared almost everything else
most of our lives. Why not the odd lover or two?'

Suddenly Mac was on his feet and leaning across the
desk, one long finger stabbing threateningly into Joel's
watchful face. 'If I find you've made a single pass at
her, Joel, so help me, I'll kill you—got that?'

Joel's eyes narrowed suddenly. 'Is that a challenge,
Mac?' he enquired softly.

'That was no challenge,' Mac harshly denied. 'It was
a clear-cut threat! Make one move on Bunny and you'll
regret it!' he warned, too angry to notice the way he had
used his very private pet name for Roberta.

Hard-as-glass silver eyes held curiously assessing
brown ones and, for the first time ever, the two brothers
looked at each other in mutual hostility.

'I don't think that's your prerogative any more,' Joel
said quietly. 'Roberta has finished with you, remember?
Unless, of course, you've managed to bully her into going
back to you?'

'I'm collecting her from here tonight,' Mac stated with
grim satisfaction, straightening up. 'And as far as you
or any other man is concerned, Roberta is mine, and
she stays mine. So keep your roving eye off my woman—
my woman!' he repeated possessively. 'Got that?'

Got it, Joel thought as he watched Mac slam out of his office without waiting for an answer. He had more than got it.

Slowly he reached out for the internal telephone. 'In here, please, Roberta,' he commanded when her rather husky voice answered, then replaced the receiver, a look of grim calculation on his face.

But the expression Roberta saw when she slunk warily into his office a moment later was the usual sardonically mocking one.

'I'm sorry, Joel,' she murmured guiltily. 'He—he sort of coerced the truth out of me.'

'Sit down,' he said.

She sat, looking like a whipped dog expecting to be kicked.

'Did he convince you to go back to him?' he demanded.

That brought her chin up. 'No, he did not!' she declared.

'That's not the way Mac tells it,' Joel remarked drily.

'Your brother can say what he likes,' she countered primly. 'He always has been too stuffed full of self-delusion.'

Joel smiled at that. 'So, what do you intend to do when he comes for you this afternoon?' he asked.

She gave a small shrug. 'I'm not going anywhere with him again,' she stated firmly.

'Sure?'

'Positive,' she said, and the cool green gaze she levelled on him showed such tough determination that Joel nodded as if she had managed to convince him at last.

'Then there is no reason why you can't have dinner with me tonight, is there?' he offered.

Roberta frowned at him, surprised by the invitation. 'I don't need consoling, Joel,' she told him, adding ruefully, 'and neither do I need protecting from him.'

No? His mocking look derided her certainty on both counts. But all he said was, 'Actually, I could do with you along tonight. I'm meeting Lou Sales from Portsmouth—and we both know what that means!' He sent her a rueful grin.

Lou Sales was an ex-ship engineer who, on retirement from the Navy, had started up his own marine-engineering company with a lot of financial backing from Maclaines. That was not the problem; the problem with Lou Sales was that he could drink any man under the table, and always insisted on trying! Joel wanted her along to keep track of discussions once he himself had gone beyond the point of understanding anything that the wily Lou was trying to get out of him!

'So, if you're not seeing Mac tonight,' Joel concluded casually, 'you can come and play buffer for me—can't you?'

He was challenging her resolve. Roberta recognised that and rose haughtily to it. 'Of course,' she agreed.

'Good,' Joel said, a gleam of something she did not really like entering his light brown eyes before he smoothly hooded it. 'Finish an hour early this afternoon, then,' he authorised, and Roberta knew that he was only suggesting it so that she would be away from here before his brother came looking for her. 'And I'll pick you up at seven o'clock.'

Mac arrived at six-thirty, just as Roberta was fresh from her bath, with her hair piled up on top of her head and her lightly perfumed body wrapped in sugar-pink towelling.

Poor Jenny was trying to hold him back at the flat door. He took one look at Roberta and started scowling. 'Tell her to let me in,' he commanded tightly.

'This is my flat, Solomon Maclaine,' Jenny inserted firmly. 'And I——'

'Tell her,' he growled.

Roberta's green eyes flickered. He meant business; it was pulsing from every pore in him. 'It's all right,' she said huskily to her friend. 'Let him come in.' It was either that or watch him explode on the doorstep, and, for all Jenny's bravery, Roberta didn't think her friend was up to a dose of Mac's real fury.

Glowering at both of them, Jenny reluctantly stepped to one side. Roberta dug her hands into the deep pockets of her wrap and moved into the sitting-room. Mac followed her grimly, pointedly shutting the door in Jenny's face.

Silence fell. Having to brace herself for what was coming next, Roberta turned to face him. At last he was beginning to look a little frayed around the edges. A dark frown intensified the brooding beauty of his eyes and his mouth was turned downwards—not sulky but tense, as though he was having difficulty holding it under some sort of control—harrowing enough to reach in and squeeze that weak part of her that loved him so badly.

'Come home,' he said gruffly.

Her heart squeezed again in wretched reply to that rough-voiced plea. But her eyes remained unmoved as they held on to his.

'No.' She shook her head, damp tendrils of silky hair clinging to her unhappy face. 'No, Mac. You and I want different things out of life. If I let you talk me into coming back, then I would be living a lie to myself, and I just can't do that any longer.'

'What lie?' he rasped, striding across the room until
he was standing right in front of her. His hand came up
to cup her cheek, the thumb sliding beneath her chin to
lift it up so that he could look fiercely into her eyes.
'You still want me,' he claimed. 'And that's no lie!'

'Yes,' she sighed, not bothering to deny it, especially
when he must be able to feel the way her pulses were
leaping at even the simplest touch from him. 'But what
do you want, Mac?' she asked him sadly. 'Me, the whole
person, with a mind and feelings to consider—or just
the body that responds so excitingly to yours?'

'My body responds to you in the exact same way,' he
countered huskily. 'You think I do all the taking, but
we take from each other. All the time, every time.' He
moved his fingers in a feather-like caress over her skin
that sent sweet sensations of delight sprinkling through
her. 'Even this,' he murmured as she let go a shaky sigh.
'Such a light caress, yet it's enough to make you quiver
with pleasure, and my fingers are tingling as if they're
touching the most exquisite substance ever.' His other
hand came up, sliding around the back of her neck to
tip her head gently. 'I only have to look at you to want
you, and I know it's the same with you. We're good
together!' he stated with soft ferocity. 'Why are you
trying to throw it all away?'

Why? Roberta closed her eyes, trying to shut out the
dark flame burning in his eyes. He was right. Every word
he had said was oh, so true! But that wasn't all of it,
was it? This wild, wanting sexual need assuaged only
one small part of her aching soul—what about the rest?

'I want more,' she told him thickly. 'I *need* more from
you, Mac.'

'More of what, for God's sake?' he ground out. 'More
of this?'

With an angry tug, he took hold of her robe and wrenched the two pieces of towelling apart to expose her shoulders and the smooth slopes of her creamy breasts. Her gasp of protest was lost in the angry way he hooked an arm around her waist to pull her lower body against him then lifted the other hand to her breasts. His fingertips only had to brush lightly across her sensitive nipples to have them springing into tight, tingling buds of life. He lifted dark and smoky, passionately hungry eyes to hers in silent challenge and she groaned, shaking her head in mute denial, her soft mouth drawn tensely back against her teeth to stop herself from responding.

It was a test. She acknowledged that as she stood stock-still in front of him and tried her damnedest to fight his deliberate onslaught on her senses. And, because she fought him, the caresses went on and on until her flesh began to quiver, her breathing so erratic that it sent her heart stuttering out of rhythm and she had to clench her whole body to stop herself giving in to the urge to let her spine begin a supple arch towards him, which would be the first sign of her impending surrender.

But she managed—managed right up until the moment when he brought his mouth into the battle. And then it became a living hell, if only because she knew she just didn't have it in her to fight those wonderful lips. And the blood began singing in her head as his tongue curled sensually around her own, her body arched, and her arms went helplessly up around his neck.

'God in heaven, woman!' he muttered hotly as he drew away from her clinging mouth. 'Don't you know we already attain the ultimate? Any more of your *more* and we'd risk dying!'

'Sex!' she choked out wretchedly, her green eyes opening to flash him a bitter look. 'Do you have to bring everything down to sex?'

'It's what we have!' he rasped. 'And a hell of a lot more than most people ever know! And you,' he warned, 'are lying to yourself if you try to dismiss all this as nothing!'

'I am not dismissing it,' she denied, her body trembling as she tried to back out of his possessive grasp. 'But on its own it isn't enough!'

'It has to be enough!' he said thickly. 'Because I can't offer you more, and you're fooling yourself if you think you can walk away from it.'

And, to prove his point, his mouth took hers with such devastating power that she melted—melted like wax on a burning candle, melted to his kiss, to the feel of his hands as they fumbled with the knot on her robe then thrust the fabric away. Melted to the raw, sensual feel of her naked flesh pressing against the roughness of his clothes. Melted as he moved his hands urgently down her body, the caress filling her limbs with a dark resonant warmth that had her clinging weakly to him as those knowing fingers glided over her baby-soft skin until they reached her hips where they curved possessively, holding her firm in front of him so that he could thrust his own hips against her in a sweet, pulsing rhythm of need.

He was as aroused as she was, and that made her melt all the more. This kiss was like no other they had ever shared—hot and hungry, so hungry that she couldn't seem to get enough of him and took his head between her hands, drawing him closer with tense, trembling fingers. The action had her body stretching, arching, a tight sting of pleasure rushing through her as her naked breasts rubbed against his heaving chest, her nipples tight and throbbing.

And she felt like easy meat to the ravaging hunter.

But, worse, she didn't care.

'You want me,' Mac claimed thickly.

'Yes.' She didn't even try to deny it. He was already caressing her so intimately that he had to know anyway. But conceding that much did not mean she liked herself for it, because she didn't, and along with the shame of knowing how easy she was for him came the burst of anger—the kind of anger born of hot, sweet passion—and on a surge of pure animal revenge she slid one of her own hands down his body to touch him, felt his violent surge of pleasure and dragged her mouth from his so that she could flare at him in triumph. 'And you want me!' she claimed, the words scraping huskily over her love-dried throat.

'I'm not the one trying to deny it,' he gritted. 'You are!'

'Oh!' she groaned as he moved his fingers in an intimate caress that set her whole body shuddering in response. 'You swine!' she whispered helplessly.

'For making you feel this good?' Mac smiled a lazy smile that was full of sensual triumph. 'I can make you feel even better,' he murmured temptingly against her parted mouth. 'Here and now, or preferably back in Chelsea, where we won't be disturbed. You only have to say the word...'

The word. The word was 'yes'—that was all—just one simple word and he would carry her away and all of this would be forgotten. It even hovered on the tip of her tongue, urged there by his knowing caresses and the devastating tenderness of his kiss.

He did an unexpected thing then. Instead of consolidating on the victory he was having over her senses, he pulled away, kissed her once more very gently on the mouth, and carefully folded her robe back around her body. Then he took hold of her hand and guided it back to his own ardently pulsing body. 'You,' he whispered roughly. 'Only you. Come home to me, bunny rabbit. Don't make me beg.'

He had her then. The deep, dark, throbbing thickness of his voice, the way he had used his own very personal pet name for her, which only escaped his lips when he was desperately aroused, the honesty with which he was telling her why he wanted her—and the plea. A plea she had never expected to hear him use—no matter how much he might want to. They all had her well and truly beaten, and she lifted her eyes to tell him so, give him whatever he wanted from her because never, ever in the twelve months she had known him had she ever heard Mac sound so utterly vulnerable.

Then the sitting-room door opened and Joel walked in. He paused, took in at a single glance just what was going on, and said in that light-voiced tone he used to goad people into reaction, 'Been priming my date for me, Mac? No need, big brother. I quite enjoy doing that kind of thing for myself.'

Roberta just stood, gasping at the unbelievable crudity in Joel's taunt, but Mac went one step further than that, his face contorting with black rage as he spun around, took one giant step towards Joel and raised his arm, with a fist clenched ready to punch him on the jaw!

'No!' she cried, leaping out to grab Mac's arm just in time to stop him landing the blow. The muscles beneath her fingers were bunched and ready, and it took the full strength of her two hands to hold him back. 'He

was only trying to rile you, Mac!' she said urgently.
'Please!' she pleaded when the muscles did not relax.

Eyes fierce with anger, he turned on her. 'You're defending him after what he's just implied?' he choked.

'Of course I'm not defending him!' she snapped. 'But
he's your brother! You don't punch your brother just
because he happened to make a rather crude joke!'

'But was it a joke?' Silver-bright eyes had narrowed
in hard suspicion. His hand closed around one of her
wrists with enough strength to make her wince as he
jerked her hard up against him. 'Has he been making a
play for you behind my damned back?'

'Of course he hasn't!' she denied, staring at him as
though he had gone stark, staring mad, but then she had
not been a party to his row with Joel earlier that day
and her 'How can you suspect such a rotten thing of
Joel?' fell on deaf ears.

'God,' he choked. 'And to think I had allowed myself
to believe it was all just the wild imagining of my jealous
mind!'

'All's fair and all that,' Joel put in, seeming to be
deliberately pouring oil on to the flames of Mac's anger.

Roberta flashed him a bewildered look, and was
shocked to see a glint of cold calculation gleaming in his
eyes. 'Stop it, Joel!' she snapped at him. 'This is not
funny!' Then, incredulously to Mac, 'You know there's
nothing going on between Joel and me!'

'No?' Mac's eyes were so bright with suspicion now
that Roberta quivered. 'Then what the hell is he doing
here, walking in as if he was expected?' he challenged
tightly.

'Perhaps because I am,' Joel inserted into Roberta's
clear hesitation. 'Expected, I mean,' he made provokingly clear. 'I'm taking Roberta to dinner.'

Mac turned on him like a rattlesnake ready to strike, one hand still wrapped around Roberta's waist in a bone-crushing grip while the other was clenching into a fist again. 'I've warned you once already today,' he bit out tightly. 'Don't make me repeat myself.'

'And I warned you too, if you remember?' Joel countered coolly.

The two men glared at each other, the hostility between them so strong that it crackled in the air around them. Looking anxiously from one to the other, Roberta let out a pained choke. 'Oh, please!' she begged. 'Don't fall out because of me! I couldn't bear it!'

For an answer Mac flicked his contemptuous gaze away from Joel and on to her. 'Get your coat,' he clipped. 'We're leaving, right now.'

'But I've arranged to have dinner with Joel tonight!' Her green eyes appealed for his understanding. 'I can't just——'

'Look!' he ground out with desperately waning patience. 'It isn't a damned choice between dinner with him or coming with me! It's me you belong to and me you're coming with right now! So get your damned coat!'

'But I'm not even dressed!' she declared, with a sense of utter disbelief that any of this was really happening.

'He doesn't need you dressed,' Joel mocked lazily. 'When has Mac ever needed a woman dressed? I would have thought that by now, Roberta, you would know and understand that——!'

Mac did hit him for that one. His fist landed on Joel's chin with enough force to send him staggering backwards a couple of steps before his legs gave out beneath him and he fell, knocking over a small table and landing heavily against the corner of it before he reached the floor.

On a horrified cry Roberta tried to go to him, but Mac stopped her, his hand tightening around her wrist to jerk her back to his side.

'Leave him,' he rasped, the anger in him pulsing out of every bunched muscle in his powerful body. 'Just go and get dressed.' He gave her an ungentle shove towards the door.

'No.'

Where it came from Roberta did not know. Certainly before Joel had come into the room she had weakened enough to do anything Mac could ask of her. But the ugliness of the scene which had ensued, plus something that Joel had just said, had brought her shuddering to her senses.

Grimly she went to kneel down beside Joel.

'What do you mean—no?' Mac demanded roughly, glaring as she gently turned Joel's face so that she could see the damage Mac had done to his jaw. His lip was split and bleeding, his jaw already turning an ugly shade of red. She found a paper tissue in her robe pocket and carefully placed it against Joel's lip.

'Just what I said,' she answered flatly. 'I'm not coming with you.'

A moment's silence followed that, as if Mac was having difficulty believing his own ears, then he said roughly, 'Because I hit the foul-mouthed swine?'

'No,' she said. 'He deserved it.' Joel grimaced at that, making no attempt to lever himself up from his huddled position on the floor. 'But he's also right, isn't he?' She lifted empty green eyes up to Mac's. 'You do only want me for my body. I'm nothing special to you and never will be, will I? I'm not coming back to you, Mac,' she concluded with dull finality.

He didn't say a word, not a single word. And the silence clattered around all three of them as he stood there, glaring at the two of them on the floor at his feet.

Then, in a voice Roberta barely recognised as his, it was so raw, Mac said, 'To hell with you, then,' and, with a last searing look at Joel, he turned and walked out of the room, shouldering aside Jenny, who had just appeared at the sitting-room door, as if she weren't there.

'My God,' Jenny gasped into the throbbing tension he left behind him. 'What's been going on in here?' Then she saw Joel, still sitting on the floor, nursing his jaw, and alarm widened her big brown eyes. 'Joel!' she cried. 'You've cut your lip!'

The front door slammed; Roberta sank weakly into a nearby chair, covering her burning eyes with a cold and trembling hand. 'Why did you do it, Joel?' she whispered thickly. 'Why did you have to rile him like that?'

'Contrary to your earlier statement today, Miss Chandler,' he drawled as he dragged himself to his feet, 'you do need protection when he's around. Or hadn't you realised that you were about to lie down and let him walk all over you yet again?'

She winced at the pointed sarcasm, the unpalatable truth in it shrivelling her insides with shame. Joel was right and she had been ready—more than ready—to do anything Mac wanted her to do.

'Which doesn't mean you had to be the one to protect me,' she cried. 'You and Mac are brothers!'

He nodded. 'And it's because I love my brother that I did what I did!'

'By deliberately goading him into hitting you?' she choked. 'By pretending you had something intimate going with me!'

'It worked, didn't it?' he countered. 'He came on to you all macho and ready to drag you off by your hair.'

She sighed impatiently, half wishing that she had never started all of this. 'I will not be a party to playing games with Mac's feelings, Joel,' she stated firmly.

'Why not?' he asked. 'He's been playing games with your feelings for long enough! No, listen to me,' he went on quickly as Roberta paled under that brutal thrust. 'Mac loves you, Roberta. He has from the first moment he laid eyes on you, only he's just too damned thick to recognise it. He needs waking up,' he stated flatly. 'And if you love him as much as you seem to do, then you'll help wake him up before he loses his last chance to gain some proper happiness in his life!'

'He's not Sleeping Beauty!' she cried, looking at Joel as if he'd gone stark, staring mad.

'Yes, he is—in a way,' Joel insisted, though he smiled at the comparison he had unwittingly made. 'Only in Mac's case he was pricked in the finger by the marriage trap, and is so damned scared of being pricked again that he daren't even look true love in the face without breaking out into a cold sweat!'

'True love!' she scoffed. 'You're the one who's blind if you really believe that. Mac doesn't want me because he loves me! He wants me because I excite him in bed!'

'And no wonder, if you flame as spectacularly in passion as you do in anger!' he drawled, hazel eyes twinkling as they ran over her own sparkling eyes, her deliciously trembling mouth and the wicked sensuality of her heaving breasts.

'Well, find some other sucker to wake your brother up,' she snapped. 'I no longer care for the job.'

Joel was silent for a moment, his eyes fixed on her bowed head while he played warily with his swelling jaw, then he said carefully, 'I suppose dinner is off too? Only Lou will be——'

Her head snapped up, her green eyes threatening to splice him in two.

'OK—OK!' he said, putting up a defending hand. 'I can see that you're too angry with Mac to eat a single morsel, so I'll just take myself off, and...' It wasn't just Mac she was angry with—and Joel knew it.

'Just get out of here, Joel,' she suggested huskily. 'Before I do something we might both regret!'

CHAPTER FOUR

'WHAT was all that about?' Jenny demanded in bewilderment once Joel had left.

'Nothing,' Roberta said wearily. 'Just Joel playing one of his sick jokes on his brother at my expense!'

'You mean it was Mac who split his lip?' Jenny gasped in disbelief.

'Well, it certainly wasn't me!' Roberta derided, then added grimly, 'But I'm now wishing it had been!'

Who did he think he was, she thought angrily, trying to interfere in her and Mac's private life? And how dared he suggest that his brother loved her?

Mac didn't know the meaning of love. He only knew the meaning of sex. And she was well rid of him! she told herself stubbornly.

But hours later, having shared a light meal with Jenny, then turned her attention to the TV set, Roberta had to admit that she wasn't watching anything. In fact, she hadn't heard or seen a single thing that the TV had been chucking at her all evening!

She was waiting, she realised. She was sitting here in a definite tense waiting mode, waiting for Mac to ring— *hoping* that he would ring! Yet hoping just as desperately that he would not.

She sighed and sighed again, wishing that these strange sensations she was experiencing inside did not make her feel so—wretched!

You're in mourning, she diagnosed her problem. Mourning a dead love.

No, not dead, she then revised that thought. But cast into a self-imposed exile. Which only made it harder to deal with, simply because she knew she was having to fight her own decision, her own feelings while knowing—well, half knowing—that Mac would take her back if she just got up now and went to him.

Mac.

Those tiny muscles deep inside her quivered, her senses beginning to ache with a wretched need just thinking about him. About the sheer masculine beauty of his dark good looks. His lazy smile. His sensual kiss. His light, knowing touch...

Her fingers twitched, then began to tingle when she remembered just where she had last touched him intimately. So warm, so strong, so potently aroused that she had to be mad to be giving up the kind of pleasure he could generate for——

'I'm going to make a coffee. Do you want one?'

Roberta blinked, the sound of Jenny's voice dropping her like a lift down ten floors as she came out of her reverie. 'I—no, thank you,' she answered huskily. 'I think I'll just go to bed...'

'OK,' Jenny accepted easily enough, but her eyes were knowing as she watched Roberta leave the room, knowing as well as Roberta did that she wouldn't sleep a wink tonight, no matter how hard she tried.

And she didn't. She lay there thinking instead. Thinking of Mac as the dynamic businessman she had first met in Joel's office only days after she joined the company. He'd looked lean, clean, sharp and alive, the well-structured shape of his body by no means disguised by the conventional navy blue suit and pale blue shirt he had been wearing.

He had been laughing with Joel when she had looked up and seen him for the first time and, like a frame taken out of time, she could still hold that picture of him with his head thrown back, his black hair shining in the overhead lights, his face lean and richly tanned because—she'd found out later—he had just returned from a month-long holiday sailing around the Bahamas with his teenage daughter. She could still see his mouth, disturbingly sensual even while wearing that amused smile. And his eyes, a soft, laughing grey that had warmed her through to her very core when they had suddenly settled on to her.

Joel had seen what was happening to her and had smiled wryly as he'd introduced them. 'Our chairman, Solomon Maclaine,' he'd introduced Mac drily. Then to Mac, 'Roberta Chandler, my new PA.'

'Bertie for short? Or even something more exotic— like Bunny?' Mac asked, stepping forward to take her hand.

'No!' she denied, struggling to maintain her composure because, even then, the simplest touch of his hand had filled her with a hot, stifling breathlessness she had never experienced before. 'No one ever calls me Bunny,' she protested. 'And I wouldn't answer to it if anyone did!'

'Except for a lover, of course,' Mac added outrageously, and watched with a kind of surprised fascination as a blush ran right up her creamy cheeks.

'Not even then,' she demurred, lowering her gaze from his because she just didn't know how to handle the messages his eyes were sending.

'We'll see,' he murmured softly.

And they had seen.

Her stomach curled, forcing her body to curl with it into a tight ball of aching misery as her memory played another picture across her mind: a picture of the two of them lying naked on a white-sheeted bed, she supine beneath him while he lay above her, his body hot and hard, sheened like silk by a fine layer of moisture, the intensity of their desire for one another so concentrated that nothing else in the world existed.

'Bunny...' she could hear him whisper, the erotic wonder in the soft, husky sound enough to tip her, groaning, right over the edge.

Then, more often than not, the phone would ring, she reminded herself staunchly. And it would be Delia or Lulu demanding his attention—and getting it as they brutally reminded him where his priorities lay.

With them, not with her. Not with his current bimbo, who was there to be used and discarded as the moment demanded!

Grimly she turned her face into her pillow, and forced herself to remember the bad side of Mac. His careless indifference to her deeper feelings. His crass selfishness in the shrugging way that he would dismiss any protest she might put up against his demanding family with a simple, 'I'm sorry, Roberta, but I have to go.' And that would be the end of that. She would revert back to being Roberta again, and the 'Bunny' he had just been so completely engrossed in would become nothing but a shadowed memory, lost behind more pressing concerns.

Heavy-eyed from a rotten night of restless battle with her emotions, and feeling bad-tempered enough to scowl at anyone who so much as glanced her way, Roberta walked into the plush executive foyer of Maclaines, ready to do battle with anyone who dared take her on!

But Joel was her ultimate target, since he, in her wretched state of mind, had become no better than Mac with his outrageous behaviour of the night before.

So she was ready for a row in more ways than one as she took the lift up to the executive floor and walked in through the doors which led to Joel Maclaine's personal suite of offices—only to have her blazing guns spiked the moment she arrived.

'Emergency—emergency!' Mitzy chanted with brisk whimsy the moment she saw Roberta. 'Joel has been called away to deal with some urgent business down Portsmouth way, and you're to go to Zurich instead of him.'

'Me?' Roberta choked. 'But I don't have the authority to sign deals for Maclaines!'

'You aren't to sign anything,' Mitzy informed her. 'Just stall them until Joel can get there in a couple of days' time.'

'But that's crazy logic!' Roberta protested. 'Franc Brunner was already turning shy on Friday afternoon. If we don't strike while the iron is hot we may lose the deal altogether.'

Mitzy just shrugged, as if that wasn't her problem, and picked up a bulky file which she held out to Roberta. 'This is for you,' she said. 'Everything to do with Brunner's is in it. Joel said you've to take it with you and sift through it with a fine-tooth comb, looking for loopholes, then use them as stalling fodder until he can get there. He reckons that Franc Brunner is pulling a fast one in the hopes of getting more money from us, and Joel is just not going to play.'

At last! Roberta thought with a deep sense of relief. At last Joel has seen the light of day!

'Brunner, he said to remind you,' Mitzy continued, 'needs us more than we need him. So a bit of cold shoulder from us right now may help remind the crafty old devil of that. So I'm to put today's meeting with Brunner back until tomorrow morning and you're booked on the lunchtime flight out of Heathrow to Zurich today, so you've got the rest of today to go through that lot.' She pointed at the file while ignoring Roberta's blank-eyed consternation. 'There's a hotel room already booked in the company name,' she went on briskly, naming one of the top international hotels, 'and you're going to have to hop to it if you want to go home and pack a bag before you catch that flight.'

'When did Joel organise all of this?' she asked in a bewildered voice.

'This morning,' Mitzy said, adding drily, 'Very early this morning—when he chased me out of bed and had me in here at six-thirty, no less, and I am not amused!'

'No,' Roberta murmured thoughtfully, 'I can see you're not. If he had to inconvenience one of us, then why didn't he have me dragged out of bed, since I seem to be the one all these orders are being thrown at?'

Mitzy just shrugged. 'Don't ask me to explain how his mind works,' she sniped. 'All I know is that, by the time I got in here, he was already running around like a demented fly. And all of that——' she pointed to the file again '—was already compiled and waiting for you.'

'So, what's happened at Portsmouth?' Roberta then enquired, remembering Joel's dinner with Lou Sales last night.

'Apparently Mr Sales has an engineering problem,' Mitzy explained. 'So Joel has gone down there to help sort it out. Which leaves me,' she then added complainingly, 'running this department all by myself!'

*   *   *

Well, perhaps it was for the best, Roberta decided as she waited to board her flight at Heathrow Airport. Falling out with Joel as well as Mac would do her no good in the end. She did, after all, have to work closely with him. And he was a good boss to work for most of the time. It was only where their relationship overlapped from business into the personal that things got complicated, and perhaps, from now on, she should make sure that it didn't happen again.

Perhaps you should have applied the same piece of advice to the company chairman! she then told herself grimly. Then you wouldn't be feeling as rotten as you're feeling right now. Which, again, probably made Zurich the best place she could be for the next few days—if only because it placed her beyond temptation where Mac was concerned. At least in Zurich she couldn't, even if she wanted to, weaken her resolve and see him.

Mac...she thought wistfully then, ruining all her good common-sense thinking by drifting off into a world dominated by the man. A man who exuded power and a menacing sexuality wherever he was or whatever situation he was in. Like in his office on the floor above her own, just sitting behind his big red leather-inlaid desk, he managed to ooze enough charisma to charge her up sexually. Or walking out of the bathroom at his Chelsea flat after an invigorating shower, so utterly at ease with his own nakedness that he would have the gall to grin at her wide-eyed, hungry stare because he knew what his nakedness did to her.

Arrogant devil, she thought now, but yearningly. Dressed or undressed he was one vibrantly sexy man. He even looked great in tennis whites, hard muscles rippling as he played with a power-house accuracy which showed how easily he could have taken the game up pro-

fessionally with a little encouragement from his parents;
he was *that* good.

But they hadn't encouraged him, and that grim conversation they had once shared in the darkness of their
bedroom one night came back to remind her. A night
when they had made love with no interruptions to spoil
the beauty of it, when she had listened to him talk, her
body curled closely into his while he told her about
himself, about his ambitions, his regrets, his secret
dreams.

She had been so sure that he was coming to love her
then; why else would he have opened himself up to her
the way he had? The way he had peppered his words
with soft, loving kisses and light touches, as though
needing to reassure himself that she was there with him
in the darkness while he talked, had confirmed as much,
his voice quiet and low, telling her things she could have
almost sworn he had never told anyone else.

Things about his early years at boarding-school, when
he had missed his parents so much that he'd had to learn
to channel his energies into something demanding or let
the rest of the boys see how pathetically homesick he
was. How it had been years later before he discovered
that they'd all felt the same way—lost, lonely, vulnerable, rejected. Some had found their succour in hard
study, others, like himself, had found it in sport. Not
that he had sacrificed his education to it. Luckily, he'd
admitted, he hadn't needed to, since a natural ability to
absorb facts and figures had helped him sail through his
academic studies with a minimum of effort so that he
could sink all of his passion into sport. Rugby, cricket,
and above all tennis.

He'd told her of his sense of pride and achievement
when he was selected to play for his county—only to

have his parents block the chance. Sport, they'd told him, was all well and good in its place. But their eldest son was destined for better things. He was heir to the great Maclaine empire, which meant anything sporty had to take a back seat.

He'd told her how sheer frustration and disappointment had made him rebel then, and she could still feel the way his small grimace had brushed against her cheek when he'd told her how, that summer of his eighteenth birthday, he had reacted by chucking all his sporting equipment into the rubbish bin and refusing point-blank to play again—even for his school. He had gone a little wild after that, not only rebelling against his beloved sport but rebelling against life itself, refusing to conform to anything, and falling into one mad gaffe after another, until the ultimate gaffe had been to make Delia pregnant.

His parents were pleased—*her* parents were pleased, since their daughter had been behaving no better than he had been behaving. It meant they could slip the reins on their wild children and tug them firmly back into line. Their marriage, he'd heavily confessed, had been a disaster almost from the moment it had begun. They'd both been too young, both had had too many other things in life they would rather be doing than playing house and being parents themselves, when they were still of an age where even the word 'parent' was enough to make them burn with resentment. Their only saving grace, he'd conceded, was that they had both adored Lulu from the very moment she was born. They had doted on her, her grandparents had doted on her. And if in private he and Delia had fought like cat and dog, in front of Lulu, or their respective parents, they'd behaved like star-crossed lovers, if only to keep hidden from

sight the misery that their recklessness had paid them
back with.

He had showed no interest in anything sporty for years
after that, then one day Joel had arrived at his door with
two tennis rackets in his hand and a boyish grin on his
face as he'd said, 'Please, Mac, will you come out and
play with me?'

Roberta heard Mac's fond laughter echo back to her
from that dark, special night, full of warm and loving
affection for his only brother.

So he had started playing tennis again—against Joel
mainly—once again using the game as succour to his
feelings, venting all the angry frustrations he had been
storing up inside because both he and Delia knew their
marriage was on the rocks but neither would make the
move to end it because they were both so reluctant to
hurt Lulu and disappoint their parents yet again.

Roberta sighed to herself. The unhappiness and frustration Mac had endured through those years had been
so palpable as he'd described them that she could still
hurt for him now as much as she had done the night he
had told her about them.

Then the crunch had come, she recalled. By then, he
and Delia were leading virtually separate lives, except
for the fact that they still lived in the same house. Mac
was being groomed to take over from his father, whose
heart condition was already a cause for concern, so he'd
found himself working all the hours God sent him in an
effort to ease his father's workload while Delia just did
her own thing, unfettered by a husband who really did
not care what that thing was so long as she was discreet
about it. Then one night he'd come home a day early
from a business trip to the States, to find Delia with
another man.

All right, he'd conceded, so he had known she took lovers, but, as far as he had been aware, she did not sleep with them in their home! And finding a strange man wandering about the place, as if he belonged there, had acted like a catalyst to ten years of toeing the line for everyone else's sake! And he'd decided that if Delia could not respect their home as a sanctuary from everything else they did apart, then he wanted no more of their marriage, so he'd moved out and filed for divorce.

No one had liked it. His parents were furious. Delia was furious because she'd quite liked the easy lifestyle their indifferent marriage offered her. And the ten-year-old Lulu had been utterly inconsolable. She'd vowed never to speak to him again, and certainly, for long, wretched months, had held tight to that vow. Then his father had had another heart attack which had proved fatal—just another burden of guilt he had to carry around with him.

It was awful, he had confessed. A chapter in his life he still had not come to terms with and would never want to repeat so long as he lived.

Which was why he was so against marriage, Roberta had concluded, and why his family still held him by the apron-strings.

'Excuse me, madam?'

Roberta blinked, bringing her eyes into focus on the smiling hostess who was leaning towards her. 'Would you fasten your seatbelt, please? We are about to land.'

Land? Roberta blinked again, stunned by the fact that she seemed to have managed to get herself on to the plane and through the whole journey without even remembering leaving Heathrow!

Mac! she blamed angrily. She had lost herself in her favourite fantasy called Mac.

* * *

She was beautiful as always, her slender curves clothed in a mint-green suit, and her pale blonde hair had every man in the near vicinity turning to admire her as she paused in front of the sea of faces flanking the arrivals bay. Not that Roberta noticed their interest. She was too busy reading the selection of call-cards being held up for the benefit of people like herself who were being met by a stranger.

Another of Joel's quick arrangements. A friend of his, he'd told Mitzy to tell her, who had promised to look after her until he could get there himself. Apparently he was to act as interpreter-cum-chauffeur for any meetings she might set up with Franc Brunner. Which did not seem at all necessary to her, since Franc Brunner spoke perfect English.

But, with a mental shrug, she asked herself who she was to question the boss's arrangements and continued scanning the row of cards, until her eyes collided with her own name, resting against the white-shirted chest of a man who, even as she walked coolly towards him, put her instincts on red alert as she read the lazy interest in his pale blue eyes.

Tall and rake-slender, the word 'handsome' went nowhere near describing his blond good looks. But what was more to the point was that the man knew it and, by the rakish pose he adopted when he saw her walking towards him, was the kind who fed on his looks for all he was worth.

She had that confirmed the moment she stopped in front of him and received a smile fit to burn the stockings of a lesser woman.

'Miss Chandler?' he enquired, with a pleasant lilt to his German accent. 'My name is Karl Loring, and I am to be your companion for the next few days.' With a discarding flourish of the call-card, he held out his hand to her instead.

Roberta took it. 'Mr Loring,' she acknowledged, 'thank you for giving up your time at such short notice.'

'My pleasure,' he smiled. 'Joel never told me he had such a beautiful assistant. I can see it is going to be my pleasure—entirely.'

The barest hint of a question in that last part made Roberta glance at him sagely. She was going to have trouble with Karl Loring if she wasn't careful, she noted grimly. The man was a charmer, through and through. And conceited enough to expect his advances to be welcome.

'Shall we go?' she suggested coolly, and was irritated to watch his pale eyes begin to gleam as he heard and understood the silent brush-off in her tone. She'd only managed to whet his appetite, she realised.

Still, he had obviously decided to hang fire for the time being because all he did next was offer to carry her small weekend bag for her, then took a light grip on her arm to guide her out of the building.

His car was a sleek, top-of-the-range white BMW, and he drove into the city with smooth efficiency, happy, it seemed, to chatter on about himself without really expecting any input from her. He was apparently an interpreter by trade but, because he came from a certain social background, his large circle of friends held places of some power in the business community which meant that he had access to a lot of supposedly classified information that he was willing to pass on for the right incentive.

Money, in other words, Roberta noted wryly. And assumed he must do quite well at it, if his car and the expensive cut of his clothes were a guide.

And she supposed that his easy charm and laid-back manner worked well on a lot of people. She frowned, wondering how Joel could have been fooled into believing the image. Eyeing Karl surreptitiously, she made herself look beyond the handsome profile to the substance beneath. There was a shrewdness about those eyes, she saw, and something about the smiling mouth that hinted at an ability for ruthlessness.

Yes, she decided. This man was clever—cleverer than she had first given him credit for. His handsome playboyish manner could just be a cloak he liked to hide behind, and his lazy charm probably got him places otherwise closed to him. She could well imagine this man being dismissed by his peers as empty and harmless, when in actual fact he was a fox. A sleek, smooth, beautifully groomed but very cunning fox.

Pulling up outside the hotel, he killed the engine, then turned that sizzling smile on her again. 'Shall we start by sharing dinner tonight?' he suggested. 'Maybe get to know each other a little better before we really have to put our minds to work tomorrow.'

Roberta frowned. 'I don't know...' she murmured uncertainly, having no wish to alienate him, even if he could become a problem. But he was a friend of Joel's, and Joel was her boss. 'I have a lot of paperwork to go through if I'm to be of any use at all here to Joel.' She posed her refusal carefully.

'All work and no play, Miss Chandler,' he chanted teasingly. 'And you have this afternoon to dedicate to work. Think about it,' he urged her huskily. 'Perhaps by tonight you will be crying out for a little light relief from your paperwork. Why not use me, and a shared dinner, for that diversion?'

His eyes, mouth, the sheer body-language of the man literally oozed sexual charm—so much so that she actually felt herself beginning to respond to it!

And why not? she suddenly asked herself belligerently. You're a free agent now! You can respond to whomever you please!

'All right, Mr Loring,' she heard herself accepting. 'And thank you for asking me.'

'Karl, please,' he invited, his eyes alight with expectancy.

Her hesitation was only slight before she returned the invitation. 'Roberta,' she informed him, and his pleased smile at her acquiescence must have been infectious because she found herself smiling too.

'Shall we say seven-thirty, then?' he suggested.

Just what I needed! she decided, when she noticed a new lightness in her step as she walked into the hotel to book in. Karl Loring might be an out-and-out rake, but even a rake was better than nothing to a girl alone in a strange city.

And anyway, she decided, it did her battered ego good to have someone as good-looking as Karl eager to be with her!

Then she frowned, making a mental note to find out if he was married, or divorced—or obligated in any way, shape or form!

She'd had her fill of men like that.

Her room turned out to be a luxury suite, which made her smile ruefully because she knew it really should not be. But it had been booked originally for Joel—and Joel obviously expected only the best.

Still, she wasn't going to complain, she decided happily as she moved about the elegant grey and green bedroom, putting away the few items of clothing she had brought with her. Then, with her mind firmly clicked on to work, she hauled the bulky file out of her briefcase, took it into the equally elegant sitting-room, plonked it down on the low table flanking two soft sofas, then sat down and began the long slog through all the paper stuffed inside, looking for those loopholes that Joel had said he wanted her to find.

It was gone five o'clock before she came up for air, and it was the sudden rumbling of her stomach that did it, reminding her that she had barely eaten a single thing all day!

She called Room Service, ordering herself a ham sandwich and a pot of coffee, then stood, looking down at the mass of papers scattered across the table. Several hours of solid reading had turned up nothing that could vaguely be called a loophole. Not that she was surprised; the people in Maclaines' legal department weren't known for leaving loopholes. Mac wouldn't employ them if they were.

Mac.

No, she told herself firmly, when the usual ache began deep down in the pit of her stomach. For the next few days she was not going to think of Mac!

She would have a quick shower instead, she decided abruptly, aware even as she moved off towards the bedroom that it was Mac's name she was moving away from.

Fifteen minutes later saw her coming out of the bathroom wrapped in one of the short, fluffy white towelling bathrobes provided by the hotel, with her hair piled up on the top of her head in a riot of silky blonde curls and her face looking pink and shiny. She moved across the room to go in search of fresh underwear to put on, then paused, a scuffling noise from the sitting-room beyond catching her attention.

Room Service! she realised, and changed direction, going to throw open the bedroom door with words of thanks ready on her lips—only to stop dead, the words congealing in her throat, when she found herself staring at not a waiter with a loaded tray, but Mac.

Mac—looking as comfortable as hell on one of her sitting-room sofas.

CHAPTER FIVE

HE WAS reclining in one corner of the sofa with the jacket to his slate-grey suit discarded along with his tie. The collar to his pale blue shirt was tugged open a couple of buttons and his feet were propped up on the edge of the coffee-table—she could hardly believe her eyes!

'Mac!' she gasped. 'What are you doing here?'

'Working—the same as you,' he drawled, obviously not as surprised to see her as she was to see him. In fact, he didn't even bother looking up from the stack of papers he had in his hand. 'What the hell has Joel been playing at with this Brunner thing, Roberta?' he demanded while she just stood there, shaking with a dreadful mixture of horrified shock and sheer, undiluted joy at seeing him. 'It's no wonder the crafty devil is still playing hard to get when we seem to have been conceding to every damned proviso he can come up with since discussions began!'

She blinked, trying to pull herself together, unable as yet to accept the fact that he was here at all, or to compute a single word he was throwing at her.

And throwing was right, she realised as her eyes began to clear, the silly rose-tinted hue through which she had been gazing at him fading away so that she could see him as he really was.

Mac was in business mode, not personal. And he was angry, his grey eyes snapping beneath frowning black brows as they flicked down the sheet of paper he was currently studying.

The Brunner deal.

Oh, goodness! She almost jumped into stinging life. Mac was going over the Brunner deal!

'Come here and take a look at these,' he commanded, still without offering her a single glance.

Fingers playing nervously with the knotted belt to her robe, she went, simply because she didn't know what else to do! Mac playing the impatient businessman was a whole new concept to her. She might work in the same building as him, and he might be her ultimate boss, but, until now, he had made a strict rule never to involve himself in any business matters that she might be involved in too!

'Concessions—concessions!' he gritted, the back of his fingers snapping against the paper in a deriding pointer to what he was talking about. 'In each one of these meetings Brunner demanded and we conceded. Sit down,' he ordered, sliding his feet to the floor so that she could get by him and sink meekly down next to him.

Impatiently he spread the papers relevant to what he was talking about out on top of the rest on the table. 'Here.' He stabbed with a finger. 'And here and here and here—all concessions he had no right to demand and we must have been mad to agree to!'

The words on the papers swam in front of her eyes, her mind rocking on the realisation that, in the fifteen minutes she had been out of this room, Mac had let himself in, made himself comfortable, then sifted through a daunting mound of paperwork to filter out every point worth criticising! Dazedly she lifted her eyes to his face, which was lean and taut in profile, seeing for the first time a side of him she had never personally witnessed before. Oh, she knew all about his razor-sharp reputation, his keen intelligence, his ability to home right in on the nitty-gritty of a problem in a way that kept all those around him dancing nervously on their toes in an effort to keep up.

But this much, in fifteen minutes? Her mind boggled.

'Patents,' she managed to utter constrictedly. 'We want the patents Brunner holds.'

'At any price?' Mac asked succinctly.

'Fibre optics is a revolutionary product, Mac, you know that.' He nodded, and Roberta moistened her lips, the fact that he hadn't snapped her head off giving her the courage to continue. 'Well, those patents Brunner is selling with the business revolutionise the revolution! He knows he can virtually ask his own price. In his shoes, you would be demanding the same pound of flesh.'

'True,' he accepted. 'But me being me, and my company being the solid institution it is, I wouldn't be selling those patents at all, would I?'

Her lowering eyes acknowledged the mockery he had just made of her argument. He was right. And the only reason Franc Brunner was having to sell was because his company was in dire financial difficulties—which made all those so-called concessions Mac was annoyed about a real mockery to good business sense.

'This whole deal is a disgraceful mess. You know that, don't you?' he prompted grimly.

Squirming a little inside, Roberta nodded. She had begun to think that way herself—weeks ago, in fact, when Franc Brunner had really begun to squeeze Joel.

'Joel has behaved like a soft touch, and that has made Brunner greedy.' Mac ruthlessly hammered the point home. 'So greedy, in fact, that even now at the eleventh hour, when everything is supposed to be settled bar an official signing, he's trying to pull yet another fast one over us. It won't do, bunny rabbit,' he murmured softly. 'It just won't do.'

Roberta stiffened, the use of that pet name and the way his hand came across to squeeze her knee waking her up at last to the reality of just who she was sitting here with.

The Boss. From the moment he had begun talking she had seen him only as the big boss, who had a right to question and criticise anything he saw fit regarding work. But suddenly he was Mac again, her lover—*ex*-lover! And she lifted wary green eyes to his.

'What are you doing here, Mac?' she demanded suspiciously.

For the first time he looked her directly in the eye—not that he was willing to give anything away with it. 'Working,' he answered coolly. 'I told you. Working—just like you.'

'But this Brunner thing is Joel's baby,' she persisted. 'You don't usually intrude on his domain.'

'Joel is in Portsmouth.'

Roberta nodded. 'I know,' she said. 'Which is why I'm here in his place.'

'Is it?'

Her stomach knotted, the darkening look in his eyes and the way he spoke those two soft words enough to drench her in a heated sense of alarm.

'Wh-what do you mean?' she demanded warily.

The hand at her knee moved to her thigh in one smooth, sinuous caress, sending sharp shards of electricity sprinkling through her body. 'What would you like it to mean?' he countered softly.

'I——' No! She jumped up, dislodging the hand and the dangerous mood he was trying to encourage. Then she turned on him furiously. 'You arranged all of this, didn't you?' she accused.

'Arranged what?' He was being deliberately obtuse, preferring to let his gaze follow the contours of her body, barely concealed beneath the skimpy robe.

'Joel's sudden disappearance to Portsmouth!' she snapped. 'My having to come here in his place! You arranged the whole damned thing!'

Mac smiled, relaxing back into the sofa so that he could run his eyes over her angry face and bright, flashing eyes. 'You're almost excruciatingly sexy when you get angry,' he observed. 'Did you know that?'

'And that,' she retaliated hotly, 'is just about the most ineffective remark you've ever made to me!'

'Ineffective, hmm?' he mused. 'An interesting choice of words—especially when your body-language says otherwise.' Mockingly he dropped his gaze to where her arms had somehow become wrapped tightly around her body, as if to contain whatever was happening beneath them.

Roberta sighed, sheer exasperation in the sound because he was right; he only had to murmur suggestive words like those to her to set her body alive. 'Just tell me why you're here,' she insisted. 'Business or pleasure? Because if you're here to deal with business, then, as you're my boss, I shall be only too willing to work with you. But if it's pleasure you're after then you can, quite frankly, go to hell.'

'Hell?' he quizzed, sublimely at ease in his relaxed position on the sofa, seemingly content to torment her with the lazy slide of his eyes. 'By the colour heating your cheeks, my sweet, it's you who's veering very close to that fiery place. Is that sensitive little place tucked between your thighs warming up too?' he questioned silkily, moving so suddenly that she gasped, both at the outrageous comment and the threatening way he came to his feet. 'Shall we see?' he murmured, reaching for her.

'Don't you dare!' Quickly she took a step back to avoid him, her arms remaining defensively clamped around her body. But even as she made the protest she felt her cheeks getting hotter and that place he was talking about begin to throb in heated response. 'I could sue you for sexual harassment if you keep this up!' she warned.

'As I could sack you for incompetence, Miss Chandler?' he countered, challenging her with the sudden narrowed gleam in his eyes. 'For the way you've helped waste company money with this Brunner deal?'

'You wouldn't!' she gasped, backing away one shaky step at a time while he followed.

'No?' he mocked. 'Didn't you have even one small concern that Joel was going over the top with his concessions?'

'I...' She floundered, her small white teeth biting down on the softened flesh of her lower lip. To admit that she had had reservations about Joel's handling of the deal would just drop Joel right in it. But to deny any concern would make her look a blind and gullible fool. Which came too close to being a bimbo for her liking.

'Joel is my boss.' She went for the compromise. 'He's the more experienced. I have to trust that he knows what he's doing.'

'Very loyal,' he commended. 'Now let's discuss this sexual harassment thing.' He reached out with a hand towards her, Roberta snapped her head back in rejection and he laughed, the warm, rakish laugh of a man who was enjoying the hunt. 'I really do think it's debatable which of us is harassing whom, you know,' he drawled.

'I mean, who's the one with hardly any clothes on here?' he challenged, with a mocking tilt to his brow.

'This is my room,' she argued. 'It's you who's infiltrated my privacy, not the other way around.'

'Wrong,' he denied, taking another step forward while she took one back. 'This *suite* is reserved in the company name. My name,' he pointed out. 'Who ever heard of a mere assistant occupying a luxury suite of rooms?'

'It—it was booked for Joel,' she defended stammeringly, seeing his trap and no way out of it.

'My brother,' Mac nodded. 'And a co-director. He's allowed the luxury perks—you're not.'

'I'll—I'll leave, then,' she said, feeling definitely cornered now, her hand lifting in a rather helpless gesture towards the bedroom while her bare feet took her another two paces back. 'J-just let me get dressed and collect my things and I'll f-find myself another room...'

'What—after making yourself so deliciously available to me?'

'I didn't!' she disclaimed.

'I've heard of women sleeping their way to the top,' he went on mercilessly, 'but it's the first time anyone's ever tried it on me.'

His eyes were gleaming with cruel mockery as she let out a choked gasp of protest.

'Don't worry,' he assured her. 'I think I might enjoy the experience. Come peddle your wares, Miss Chandler,' he invited, 'and let's see.'

'No!' she choked. Then, because she couldn't stand it any longer, 'Oh, stop it, Mac! Stop—stop *playing* with me!'

He laughed, then caught her—not surprisingly, since he could have done so at any time in the last few minutes. 'OK,' he murmured as his arms closed around her.

'Withdraw the harassment charge on me and I'll withdraw mine on you,' he offered.

Angry, because she knew he had her well and truly beaten, she glared up at him, wondering violently how badly her fist would suffer if she smashed it against his jutting jaw! His grey eyes were laughing, knowing exactly what she was thinking and challenging her to try it.

So neither moved, both waging this particular battle with their eyes, until the air around them began to sizzle, and something else began to take the place of anger— something even more provoking, something so darkly sexual that her skin began to tingle—tingle so badly that she began to feel like a firework, lit and ready to explode.

The room disappeared, the furniture with it, until all that was left was herself and Mac, and the new sensations buzzing between them that were so sexually stimulating. She knew he only had to bend his head and kiss her for her to go up in a shower of crackling flames.

Mac—this is Mac, her senses were whispering to her. The man we love to look at, smell, touch, taste——

The pink tip of her tongue appeared, making a slow, anxious circle of her parted lips. Mac's eyes dipped to watch the revealing motion, the irises softening into such a dark and smoky grey that she was breathless suddenly, knowing what she was inviting but utterly unable to do anything about it.

'Want me to kiss you, bunny rabbit?' he murmured softly.

She quivered, hating him for making her feel like this, but loving the tender sound of her special name on his lips. And yes, she wanted him to kiss her. She wanted him to pick her up in his big, strong arms and carry her into the other room where the bed awaited them. She wanted to strip off his clothes and lick his skin. She wanted to tangle her limbs with his, couple their bodies and die like that—die in the arms of the man she loved!

God, she thought wretchedly, what am I thinking?

A knock sounded at the door then, making Mac's grasp on her loosen as his head went up in surprise. Taking her chance while she had it, Roberta slipped away from him, running decidedly shaky fingers down her skimpy robe as she went to answer the door.

It was a waiter, who walked in carrying the tray of sandwiches and coffee she had completely forgotten she had ordered. He glanced furtively from her hot face to Mac's rueful one, then quickly hooded his eyes, too experienced in these kinds of situations not to know that he had just interrupted something very intimate.

Moving towards the low table standing between the two elegant sofas, he then paused when he saw that it was scattered with papers. Roberta jumped to make a space for the tray and as he put it down the rich aroma of freshly brewing coffee assailed her nostrils, making her swallow thirstily on the sudden surge of saliva to her mouth.

'Here.' Mac walked over to the waiter, holding out a bank-note. The man's eyes lit up as he took it, bowing in humble thanks before quickly letting himself out of the room.

'Look,' Roberta demanded in a tight voice. 'Is this suite supposed to be yours? Because if it is I'll pack my things up and——'

'Oh, yours—yours,' Mac answered casually. 'I have another one on the floor above.'

'Then I would prefer it if you left with the waiter,' she informed him pointedly.

'Without us having the chance to finish our—business?' he drawled, then bent his attention to the loaded tray that the waiter had placed on a free corner of the coffee-table. 'Mmm,' he said as he lifted the cover off the plate of delicately made ham sandwiches. 'Refreshments while we talk shop. Good girl,' he murmured as he sat down and took one. 'I'm starving.'

'I didn't order them for you,' she snapped, then sighed when he just bit into the sandwich with overplayed relish and settled back to make himself comfortable.

'All right.' Convincing herself that it would do her no good to antagonise him when this Brunner deal was in such an obvious mess, she made herself sit down on the other sofa and poured herself a desperately needed cup of coffee. 'Let's talk business.'

'I wouldn't mind a coffee myself,' Mac prompted.

'There's only one cup,' she pointed out, feeling a petty sense of triumph at being able to say it.

'So, I'll use yours when you've finished with it,' he shrugged, and took another sandwich, then, with a wicked gleam in his eyes, lifted the plate and offered them to her.

Ignoring it, she asked him coolly instead, 'What do you want me to do about the Brunner deal?'

'Nothing,' he said. 'Exactly nothing,' he elaborated carelessly.

Roberta frowned. 'Is that why you're here?' she demanded. 'Are you going to see to it yourself?'

'No. As you said yourself, this is Joel's baby. He got himself into this mess and he'll get himself out of it—and answer to me later.'

'But Joel isn't here and you are,' she pointed out. 'There's a meeting scheduled with Frank Brunner in the morning. What am I supposed to do if Joel isn't here?'

'What did he tell you to do?'

'Stall.' She shrugged. 'Find out what else Brunner wants, then just stall him until Joel arrives.'

'Then that is what you must do,' Mac said.

'But with you here there's no reason for us to stall!' she cried. 'Mac,' she urged, 'you saw for yourself the mess this is all in! You could straighten it all out in ten seconds flat! You know you could!'

'Thanks for the vote of confidence,' he grinned.

'That wasn't the point I was trying to make!' she snapped, irritated by his laid-back manner. 'Joel is your brother! He's younger—far less experienced at these things than you! If he lets Brunner talk him into yet more concessions, then you know he's going to get a hell of a rocket from the board when they eventually see the final contract!'

'And from its chairman, come to that,' he agreed.

Roberta jumped to her feet, infuriated by his distinct lack of feeling where Joel was concerned. 'I can't believe you're going to stand back and watch your own brother drop himself right in it!' she cried.

'How long have you known that this deal wasn't going as well as it should?' he asked.

'I——' Damn, they were back to that again. 'What made you suddenly suspicious enough to come and check it out?' she countered smartly.

'Joel was altogether too uncomfortable on Friday night when I brought it up,' he replied. 'And you didn't look so pleased about it yourself.'

'It wasn't the Brunner deal I was displeased with,' she reminded him. 'It was you!'

'Want to kiss and make up?' he invited.

Roberta's chin went up. 'No, I do not!'

'Have dinner with me, then,' he suggested slyly, 'and we'll discuss both issues—your forgiving me and my helping my brother get out of the hole he's dug himself.'

She shook her head, glad that she had a valid excuse to refuse him. 'Sorry,' she said, 'but I already have a dinner engagement tonight.'

His eyes suddenly shot daggers at her. 'Who the hell with?' he demanded. 'You've only been in Zurich for five damned hours!'

She shrugged, secretly pleased that she'd managed to annoy him. 'A friend of Joel's,' she told him coolly.

'Joel,' Mac muttered between clenched teeth. 'I might have known he'd—— What's his name?' he then demanded.

'Karl,' she said. 'Karl Loring.'

'Break it,' he commanded tightly, the name having a strangely murderous effect on his eyes.

She shook her head, savouring her cup of coffee. 'I'm afraid I can't do that,' she said, becoming more at ease the more angry he got.

'You will if you want me to sort out the mess for Joel,' he growled.

Roberta looked sagely across the coffee-table at him. 'I should like to think that you would do that for Joel's own sake, Mac.'

His eyes darkened fractionally, but it had nothing to do with a guilty conscience for using his brother against her like this; it was sheer frustration that she wouldn't jump to his autocratic bidding.

'How did you meet him?' he asked.

'Karl collected me from the airport,' she explained, the small smile which came to play about her mouth when she recalled that meeting seeming to shoot Mac's temper right to its limits.

'Fancy him, do you?' he enquired bitterly. 'See him as the kind you can seduce into marrying you where I wouldn't?'

That hurt—hurt so deeply that she had to fight to squash the need to wince. 'What's the matter, Mac?' she countered silkily. 'Don't you like the idea of another man knowing me as intimately as you do?'

In a sudden burst of fury he shot up, his hand snaking out to take the cup from her before he hauled her to her feet. 'Don't even let yourself think about it!' he warned her bitingly. 'Or, so help me, Bunny, I'll——!'

'Don't you dare threaten me!' she flared, holding his murderous gaze with her own. 'I can eat with and *sleep* with whom I damned well like! We are finished, remember?'

'Finished?' he grated deridingly. 'You must be joking!' And to prove it he brought his mouth down punishingly on hers.

By the time he released her she was wilting like a limp rag. Mac pushed himself away from her in disgust—self-disgust, she suspected, knowing he had seen the way the tip of her tongue had flicked out to catch the droplet of blood where his angry assault had broken the delicate flesh of her bottom lip.

He turned away from her, his shoulders hunched in angry contempt. 'OK,' he said grimly. 'I'll do a deal with you, Roberta. I'll sort out this mess with Franc Brunner for Joel the moment you agree to return our relationship to the way it was.'

For a few short seconds she just stared at him in blank disbelief of what she thought she'd just heard. Then, 'Sleep with you, you mean? Why, you utter unprincipled swine!' she choked. 'What an offensive proposition to make!'

'Why?' he sighed out frustratedly. 'We've been sleeping together almost every night for a year! Why the hell should the idea of our sleeping together again be suddenly so offensive to you?'

'Because I refuse to sleep with anyone just to clinch a business deal!' she cried. 'My God,' she whispered, turning white with distaste. 'You make me feel like a whore!'

'You are not a whore!' he roared, shooting around to face her with an angry jerk.

'No?' she choked. 'Then why are you trying to treat me like one? Or do you have another name for women who use their bodies as bartering tools? Oh, go away, Mac!' she choked, on the first sob that she feared was going to be one of many. 'Just go away and leave me alone!'

With that she ran, stumbling into the bedroom to close and lock the door so that he couldn't follow her.

He didn't. He didn't even try. And, oddly, that hurt her just as much as everything else he did hurt her these days.

You're a fool, she told herself sternly. A stupid fool for letting him get to you the way he does!

So sheer defiance of her own feelings made her get herself ready for dinner with Karl. Dressed in a short, slinky dress of rich mulberry silk, her hair rearranged into the same bubbly curls on the top of her head, she waited until the very last moment before warily unlocking the bedroom door and stepping out to confront Mac again.

Only he wasn't there. And as she stood there, staring at the neatly stacked pile of papers on the table, she could not stop and, strangely, did not want to stop the great wave of emptiness that washed over her.

*　*　*

Surprisingly, because she just hadn't expected it to be, dinner with Karl was quite a pleasant experience. Mainly because Mac did not put in an appearance as she'd half expected him to. And, having spent the first half-hour constantly looking around them in case Mac did show his face, she then found herself feeling perversely irritated that he had not come to spoil the evening for her!

So perhaps it was defiance that made her respond to Karl's practised manner as he set out to charm, tease and flirt with her over the dinner-table. Or maybe it was because she found it surprisingly pleasant to be made love to in such a public place, with half the room watching them enviously while they pretended not to notice the frequent glances sent their way.

They made a striking couple, she supposed. Both blonde, both attractive, both dressed to kill—he in the dark silk lounge-suit that fitted his long, lean frame so beautifully, and she in her mulberry silk that she knew did so much for the creamy texture of her skin.

She laughed at his teasing and pouted at his more suggestive remarks. Ate delicious food and drank an even more delicious blood-red wine. And, in general, allowed defiance free rein over how she responded—if only because she was determined that if Mac should happen to walk into the restaurant he would see just how much enjoyment she could have in the company of another man.

Whatever, light-headed from too much wine and stroked into an easy mood of acquiescence by Karl's warm and amusing company, she agreed to remove to another room where a small band was playing lazy blues for the couples moving together on a dimly lit dance-floor.

'You have the most sensually alluring body I have ever held in my arms,' Karl told her as they swayed to the lazy music.

'Have I?' She turned her head a little to look up at him. 'Thank you,' she murmured huskily. 'That was a very nice thing to say.'

His blue eyes darkened. 'I would like to say a lot more to you, Roberta,' he returned deeply. 'But not here. Not in this place with all these people looking on and envying me the most beautiful woman here.'

She knew what he was suggesting, knew with a niggling sense of guilt that she had been all but asking for it through her own behaviour all evening. And as she stood there, enclosed in Karl's arms with his blue gaze sinking sensually into her own, she found herself wondering just what it would be like to have this man make love to her.

She liked Karl. She liked looking at him, she liked the feel of his hands on her back and the way her body brushed against him as they moved; she even liked the idea of feeling his mouth against her own. But would she like him making love to her? Undressing her? Touching her where only one man had ever touched her?

The hand suddenly fixing itself around her upper arm sent the hot, tingling sting of elation rushing through her and, at the same moment, gave her the answer to her question.

'Excuse me,' a cool voice intruded.

Roberta closed her eyes.

Mac. Of course it was Mac.

CHAPTER SIX

'MINE, I think,' he said as smoothly but firmly he pulled Roberta out of Karl's arms.

'Mac,' she whispered pleadingly, cheeks flushing when she sensed, from both the icy tone of his voice and the painful grip he had on her arm, a scene beginning to brew. 'You——'

His arms closed right around her, staking claim of possession right down to the way his mouth brushed away any words she was about to say. 'Sorry I'm so late, darling,' he murmured. 'But I was held up longer than I expected to be.'

What do you think you're playing at? her angry green gaze demanded.

What the hell do you think? his angry expression replied, daring *her* to make a scene by denying his right to be so possessive. A moment's battle with their eyes, with the tension beginning to flow between them, not all due to this particular situation, and she lowered her eyes, the sound of lazy music and the fact that they were not alone on the small dance-floor making her uncomfortably aware of the interest they were causing and forcing her to concede the battle to him.

Another kiss brushed her mouth, consolidating his victory, and she wanted to slap his arrogant face! He knew it, too, because she heard him utter a soft laugh, then, 'Aren't you going to introduce me to your—companion, darling?' he prompted silkily.

'This is Karl Loring,' she reluctantly complied. 'A friend of Joel's and my interpreter while I'm here in Zurich. Karl——' she lifted uncomfortable eyes to him, not surprised to find him studying them both narrowly '—this is Solomon Maclaine. Joel's brother,' she added, quite unnecessarily, she realised almost immediately, because she had only had to mention Mac's name for Karl to stiffen up in recognition, but she finished the introduction anyway. 'And, of course, my——'

Boss, she had been going to say, but Mac pre-empted her. 'I think Mr Loring understands exactly what I am to you, darling,' he mocked, and turned his attention to Karl while Roberta struggled to control the hot flush of mortification trying to mount her cheeks. 'Nice to meet you at last, Mr Loring,' he acknowledged, with an amiable nod of his dark head. 'My brother has spoken of you, of course.'

Karl returned the gesture with his head, and Roberta noticed curiously that he had gone quite pale. 'I was not aware that you were in Zurich, Mr Maclaine,' he murmured softly.

'No?' Mac frowned. 'I'm surprised that Joel never mentioned the change in plan to you... Still,' he added after a thoughtful moment, 'I don't suppose he would when my reasons for being here are purely personal—which reminds me——' he smiled '—thank you for taking care of Roberta this evening.' That rueful grin touched his mouth. 'She hates it when I have to place her second over business, don't you darling?' he added, to reinforce the rotten gibe.

She tried to pull away from him, but he stopped her by tugging her close into his side, strong fingers increasing their claim to possession by settling along her ribcage right beneath the swell of her breasts. 'But I'm

here now.' He glanced down at her hot and angry face.
'So stop pouting,' he scolded softly. 'I'll make it up to
you later.'

He was treating her like some—some empty-headed
bimbo! And fury shot like silver lances into her green,
green eyes. Mac fielded the look with a mocking one,
sleek black brows arching in challenge for her to dare
deny a single word he had said.

She couldn't and he knew it. Mac was her boss, after
all. To show him up as an over-presumptuous fool would
mean showing up the whole Maclaine empire as the same.
She couldn't do it, and lowered her head instead so that
Karl would not see the mutinous frustration burning in
her eyes.

But Mac was having none of it. He wanted his pound
of flesh from her, and was determined to get it. So once
again she felt that possessive hand tug at her slender
body, shifting her even closer to his hard-packed frame.
'Say thank you nicely to Mr Loring for looking after
you this evening, Roberta,' he prompted silkily. 'It's late
and I'm—tired.'

God, I hate you! she thought viciously, and had to
fight to lift her embarrassed face to Karl's still pale one.
'Thank you,' she said dutifully, then rebellion struck and,
instead of offering him her hand as good manners demanded she do, she leaned away from Mac to place a
light kiss on Karl's stiff cheek. 'Sorry to have to cut our
evening so short,' she murmured as she drew away.

Instead of taking some gratification from her gesture,
Karl reacted as if he had been shot, jerking his head
back from her and staring at Mac as though he expected
the other man to punch out his lights.

'No problem—no problem,' he quickly reassured her.
'Mr Maclaine is quite right and it is late. And I have a

few phone calls to make before I...' He floundered, and Roberta stared at him in angry frustration. Coward, she thought bitterly. Mac stakes his claim and you back right off! So much for your macho image! 'Nice to have met you, Mr Maclaine.' Warily he stuck out a hand towards Mac. 'No doubt we will meet again tomorrow?' Mac's brows rose in enquiry. 'F-for the meeting with Franc Brunner,' Karl elucidated.

Mac didn't answer, and whatever passed between the two men via their eyes made Karl go even paler and make his exit so hurriedly that Roberta scoffed out a sound of scorn as she followed him contemptuously with her eyes.

'If he breaks into a run, I think I shall be sick!' she muttered disdainfully, turning her attention back to Mac.

Mac's eyes were narrowed as he too watched Karl's hurried exit. 'Like he said,' he murmured thoughtfully, 'he needs to make a couple of phone calls.'

'At this time of night? To whom?' she derided scathingly. 'He's running because of your clever hands-off-my-property tactics!' She glared furiously up at him. 'When are you going to accept that I mean it when I say I don't belong to you any more?'

'Come here,' he murmured.

'No.'

'Yes,' he insisted, and drew her into his arms, moving her smoothly into rhythm with the music, his dark head lowering until his mouth hovered softly against her ear. 'My woman, bunny rabbit,' he whispered. 'Mine, whether you want to be or not.'

'How typically arrogant!' she snapped.

'How typically you, that you fight with your tongue while your body curls so deliciously into mine.'

Startled, she went still, only then aware of how in-
stinctively her arms had curved around his shoulders,
her body arching towards his.

'Damn you,' she muttered, and pulled away. 'I'm
going to bed,' she announced, turning to walk off the
dance-floor.

'Good.' Mac's arm came comfortably across her
shoulders. 'I'm coming with you.'

'Not to my bed, you're not,' she informed him. 'I was
actually enjoying myself tonight until you came along!'
she sighed out frustratedly as they reached the waiting
lift.

'I noticed,' he drawled as he lifted an arm to stop the
lift doors closing while he ushered her inside.

His sudden change in tone alone made her glance
sharply at him. 'You were watching us!' Roberta accused, seeing the sudden angry glint in his narrowed eyes.

'Right from opening to grand finale,' he mocked,
stabbing a hard finger at the lift console then leaning
his shoulders back against the wall as the door slid shut.
He fixed her with a bitter look. 'So I also saw the way
you looked at him,' he said tightly. 'And the pleasure
you found dancing in his arms! And—goddammit,
Roberta,' he exploded suddenly, 'but I also saw you
wondering just what it would be like to take him to your
damned bed!'

'That's a lie,' she cried, giving him back look for angry
look.

'Is it?' he clipped. 'You mean you didn't wonder—
just once—what it would be like to have him as your
lover instead of me?'

'I——' God, had she been so obvious? Colour surged
into her cheeks. Never a good liar, she found she couldn't

lie now, even when it was none of his business what she was thinking!

'Well, let me tell you something, sweetheart,' he murmured grimly. 'You'll never know. Not if you value your job in my company, that is.'

'What—what do you mean?' she questioned warily, not liking the dangerous look in his eyes.

'I mean,' he said, 'that Karl Loring is right off the agenda where you are concerned—and that,' he added threateningly when she went to protest, 'is an order, direct from your chairman—not just the jealous lover.'

'Ex-lover,' she corrected mutinously.

'It will be ex-chairman to you, too, if you disobey me on this, Roberta. I am that serious. Karl Loring is out, or you'll be out of my company. It's as cut and dried as that!'

And that, she made thorough note, was the boss in him speaking. A boss who never said a word without meaning it.

The lift stopped, the doors sliding smoothly open, which was a good job because it gave her something to do with her frustration—she could stalk out into the hallway and storm along to her room.

He was right behind her. Of course he was right behind her! she acknowledged angrily. This was Solomon Maclaine, and nothing fazed him, not even the withering look she had sent him before she left the lift!

'I told you...' she began to protest when he was still right behind her as she opened her suite door.

'And I told you,' he countered, his hand at the base of her spine, propelling her into the room so that he could follow.

Literally seething with angry frustration, she rounded on him. 'Just because you pay my wages, Mr Maclaine,' she began furiously, 'it doesn't mean you can——'

He walked right past her, grim indifference to anything she might want to say scored into his arrogant face as he walked across the room then paused by the low coffee-table. 'Where is the Franc Brunner file?' he asked.

'I—— Locked away in my briefcase,' she told him, momentarily stumped by his quick change from angry lover—*ex*-lover—to grimly focused businessman.

'Get it,' he commanded.

Frowning in confusion, she went to fetch it from the bedroom. 'I thought you said you weren't going to get involved with this deal,' she said as she came back.

'There were a few provisos attached to that statement, if I remember correctly,' he mocked. 'But,' he then added grimly, 'things have changed. And neither of us is getting involved with it.'

'What do you mean?' she asked as he reached for the file.

'Quite simply what I said,' he answered shortly. 'Two can play at Franc Brunner's little game. And from now on neither you nor I are available for talks, meetings or anything for the next few days.'

'But I have a meeting all set up with Brunner tomorrow, and Karl is——'

'Cancel,' he said. 'Cancel both. And don't do it yourself,' he added as an afterthought. 'Get Reception to do it for you. I want no contact—none whatsoever—between you and Loring or Brunner.'

'But—Karl is on our side, Mac,' she reminded him confusedly. 'Why play footsie with him?'

'Karl Loring is certainly not on our side, Miss Chandler,' he corrected quietly. 'Karl Loring is on Karl

Loring's side. He's in cahoots with Franc Brunner, probably on commission, so it's in his best interests to get the most he can out of us before Brunner signs anything. Joel and Loring were friends in their college days. When Brunner began to set this deal up Joel contacted Loring to pick his brains over Brunner's reputation. Loring saw instantly that he had a chance at getting in on this deal so he offered his services—to both men. His ultimate goal being to line his own pocket, of course.'

'You mean,' Roberta gasped in horror, 'that Karl Loring has actually been using his friendship with Joel to squeeze as much out of him as he could?'

Mac nodded, his attention seemingly fixed on the stack of papers he was busily sifting through. 'The first rule of survival in the world of big business, Roberta, is never to trust anyone, not even your friends. Joel knows that,' he added grimly. 'But he conveniently forgot that rule with Loring and deferred to his friendly advice right the way along the line.'

Feeling a bit as though she had just been knocked down by a steamroller, Roberta sank into the nearest chair, trying to work out how Mac had come by that conclusion when as far as she had seen there was nothing—nothing—to make him suspect such a thing!

'I don't see how you can possibly know all of this for sure,' she murmured dazedly in the end.

'Quite easily,' Mac said. 'Last night I went round to Joel's flat to thump him again for trying to move in on you, and——'

'Oh, you didn't hit him again, did you?' Roberta put in concernedly.

To her surprise, Mac smiled. 'He was too damned drunk to punch,' he told her ruefully.

'Lou Sales,' she remembered, and found herself smiling with him.

'But while he was rambling on about you, me, him and a lot of other stuff I didn't for one moment understand he also managed to show his concern for this deal,' he explained. 'And the mess he knew he was making of it.'

'So, you're here expressly to sort this all out for Joel?' she demanded, beginning to feel the first rumbling of hard suspicion.

'Of course,' he answered smoothly.

'Yet you've been refusing to help me sort it all out!' she cried. Then another thought hit her, narrowing her eyes and making her hands clench angrily at her sides. 'Why am I here, Mac?' she demanded quietly.

Mac glanced at her, and that was all it took for the very last penny to drop home. 'You're here as my hands-on assistant,' he mocked. 'Anything to say to that, Miss Chandler?' he enquired provokingly.

'That depends,' she came back stiffly, 'on whether I'm talking to my boss or the man I used to go to bed with.'

'Oh, your lover, darling,' he drawled lazily, making a fine but clear distinction between her past tense and his present. 'Most definitely your lover.'

'Then you're nothing but an unscrupulous rake!' she flared, beginning to seethe with just about every angry emotion she possessed.

'Rake?' he choked. 'What have I just said that could even vaguely be described as rakish?'

He was laughing at her, relaxed again, enjoying himself at her expense. His eyes had turned a warm and appealing shade of grey, his mouth twitching with that little smile that always got to her, no matter how angry with him she was.

'Then why else have you got your ex-lover——' it was her turn to labour the distinction '—here, if not to have your rakish way with her?'

'Rakish.' He shook his head, still laughing at her. 'I love it.'

'Don't come near me!' she warned as he began walking towards her.

'Why not?' he challenged, still coming.

'Because you're too damned sure of yourself for your own good.'

'Sure enough to know that I can make you feel wonderful if you give me a chance,' he murmured, reaching her. 'I've got a bargain for you,' he said as his arms closed around her. 'How would you like three whole days of my undivided attention playing tourist while we take avoiding action against Brunner?'

'For what purpose?' she demanded suspiciously, knowing that this man never suggested anything without an ulterior motive.

'For the purpose of enjoying each other's company, of course,' he answered, then drew her closer to him. 'Doesn't it appeal just a little bit, bunny rabbit?' he murmured, his lips brushing temptingly against hers. 'Three whole days of my undivided attention ladled solely upon you?'

'I thought you had more pride than to chase after a woman,' she pouted as a deliberate goad, but really his tenacity was warming her all the way through. Perhaps he did care for her? Perhaps he even cared more than he actually realised himself?

Strangely, he smiled, his eyes softly amused as they gazed deeply into her own. 'What's my pride worth when gauged against—this...?' he murmured as he caught her mouth.

'This' was sweet, it was gentle and it reached right down deep inside her and coiled itself tightly around every pleasurable sensor she possessed. His mouth was warm and tender, his tongue moist and exquisitely languid as it joined with her own. His hands were lightly caressing flesh that preened to his touch. She sighed softly, wishing she could hate him and knowing she couldn't, and on an act of defeat her arms slid up his arms and around his neck, fingers closing into his hair to bring his mouth more thoroughly on to her own.

'Say yes,' he urged against her searching mouth.

'Oh, God,' she choked, despising herself for being so easy for him. 'Yes, damn you, Solomon Maclaine—yes!'

On a soft growl of triumph he gathered her into his arms, his mouth fixed hungrily on to hers as he carried her through to the bedroom.

Her clothes were removed by expert hands, hands that knew just where to touch and how to touch to arouse her. By the time she had removed his jacket, tie and shirt, she was lost in the magic that was his alone—his body, his kisses, his tightly muscled flesh where her hands could run at will.

Only once did sanity briefly raise its head to warn her that she was wrong letting this happen. 'Mac,' she whispered protestingly against his mouth.

But he pre-empted her, pushing her gently down on to the bed and following her with his body, hot and hard. 'You want this, Roberta,' he stated grimly. 'We both do, so much, we ache.'

He was oh, so right, she acknowledged when, to prove it, he ran his hands down her body, caressing her where he knew so well that she couldn't help but arch and groan with desire. 'See?' he murmured, sliding his mouth sensuously against hers. 'Your body's crying out for me.

You want to feel my mouth close around your breasts and suck—suck hard until you can't tell the pain from the sheer pleasure of it.' She gasped as he did just that, lowering his head to close his lips around one throbbing peak, his tongue flicking greedily around it before he sucked it deeply into his mouth.

Her soft cry as pleasure ripped through her accompanied her fingers clutching at his head to hold him to her as she thrust upwards in a sensual need for more. He gave it, shifting to the other breast, ravishing it, driving her so crazy that she had to pull hard at his hair, bringing his head up before she actually lost all control there and then.

Triumph glowed in his eyes as he looked down on her, because he knew just how powerfully he affected her. But he was affected too; she could feel it in the hectic pumping of his heart, see it in the darkened tautness of his face and the way his flesh quivered across tightly packed muscle, as desperate to feel her touch as her flesh needed his. And, as if he knew what she was thinking, he acknowledged it, trailing a hand down her stomach to her navel, then further, until he'd dipped into the hot, moist core of her.

'Mine,' he whispered possessively. 'My woman, do you hear? Mine and no one else's. God!' he choked then, on a sudden upsurge of impassioned possessiveness. 'Never anybody else's!'

He took her mouth again, drawing her into the kind of kiss that drugged the senses while he aroused her with an urgency that actually managed to shock her. Hands, mouth, tongue, the pulsing dominance of his tightly muscled flesh so beautifully, excruciatingly sensual that she became too lost to do anything other than follow where he led.

Her body became a puppet, coaxed to respond to his
slightest touch. And she revelled in the response she urged
from him—the quickening rise and fall of his chest beneath her caressing fingertips, the rasping hiss of his
breath when she ran them along his groin, teasing him
by avoiding contact with that hard, throbbing core of
him that thrust urgently against her thigh until he could
stand the teasing no longer and grabbed one of her
hands, forcing it hard down on to him while he punished
her by drawing on her breasts again, drawing and
drawing until she cried out in wretched protest.

He knew what she wanted—needed from him even
before her legs parted to urge him between them. But
for some reason of his own Mac was holding back, his
breathing fierce as he held himself away from her a little,
supporting himself on arms which shook while he looked
into her passion-dazed eyes.

'What do you want?' he demanded gruffly.

'You,' she whispered. 'I want you, inside me, filling
me. I want you!' She tried to capture his mouth but he
wouldn't let her, the swollen power of his manhood
brushing so tantalisingly close to its goal that her senses
squirmed in frustration. 'Please, Mac—please!' she
begged.

'Now, tomorrow and all the other tomorrows—will
you still want me then?'

'Yes, oh, yes!' she groaned, too delirious to think
about what she was saying or, more to the point, what
he was asking of her. 'Forever. I love you—you know
that.'

He shuddered violently as if her answer had reached
in and touched something deep inside him, then he thrust
himself inside her, filling her as she'd so desperately
needed him to do, and her legs wound tightly around

his hips, her arms going around his neck to pull his mouth hungrily down on to hers. And, fused together like that, they began to move.

It was slow and it was strong, their flesh at one with their driving senses as they climbed towards that ultimate goal where everything would shatter in a crescendo of sheer out-of-body pleasure.

Their breath shattered first, followed by their minds, then the pulsing, throbbing collapse of everything physical. And it went on and on, holding them totally captive by the most powerful and prolonged climax they had ever shared.

Coming back to reality was not easy, or quick. Roberta was feeling shaken by it all, and she guessed that Mac was feeling very much the same himself. But, as their muscles slowly relaxed and their breathing took on a steadier pace, he lifted his head from the moist heat of her throat where it had lurched when his control had finally left him, and said thickly, 'You are the most self-lessly giving woman I've ever known, do you know that?'

'Thank you,' she whispered, loving him—unable to stop herself loving him. She understood that now.

'No.' He shook his dark head. 'I thank you, for just being what you are to me. Thank you,' he repeated gruffly again, then captured her mouth with a kiss so utterly sweet that for some crazy reason it made her want to cry.

Yet she didn't, and the reason why came in the next moment when the telephone by the bed began to ring. Mac muttered something and went to move away, but she stopped him, a foreboding the like of which she'd never experienced in her life before making her cling to him in panic.

'No,' she pleaded anxiously against his lips. 'Leave it.'

'I can't,' he groaned. 'It might be important.' But his mouth was soft and hungry against hers as he said the words, and when she wrapped her arms around his neck and moved sensually against him he shuddered, his hands sliding down the length of her, long fingers possessive and trembling, and Roberta felt a hot flood of elation as he gripped hold of her hips hard and thrust himself against her, already aroused, even after what they had just shared.

Then, with their mouths still fused, he levered himself away from her. 'One minute,' he promised against her clinging lips. 'Just one short minute, darling, please.' And he prised himself free.

His hand was not quite steady as he lifted the receiver from its rest. 'Yes?' he bit out, while his eyes, so dark and slumberous with satiation and new desire, devoured her where she lay, touching distance away from him. She quivered and he saw it happen, the hot flush of passion darkening his cheeks. And it only hit her at that moment that this was her room, and therefore her telephone to answer. She was about to say as much to Mac when, on a sudden flash of irritation, he sat up and swung his feet to the floor, then shot tensely to his feet.

'Lulu?' he muttered sharply. 'What the hell are you doing ringing me here at this time of night?'

And whose damned phone it was dropped right out of her mind as she felt her heart drop like a stone to her feet. Lulu, she was repeating over and over to herself. Of course, it had to be Lulu. Who else could possess this kind of perfect timing other than Mac's own dear Lulu?

He listened while Roberta lay perfectly still, feeling the goose-bumps come out all over her flesh as harsh reality slowly returned.

'Do you mean to tell me,' Mac said tightly, 'that you've called me long-distance just to tell me that Delia is ill?'

Delia. Lulu and Delia. Not just one of them intruding, but both.

'What? When?' His voice had deepened and grown husky with concern. 'All right, darling. Don't cry. She'll be fine, baby, be sure of it,' Mac murmured soothingly. 'An appendix operation isn't that worrying these days... No, of course I care!' He sighed in exasperation at something Lulu must have said. 'But your mother is not my responsibility any more! I have things to do here that——'

Another sigh and his beautiful shoulders were ramrod-stiff, his dark head thrown tensely back on his taut neck. What was she demanding of him, Roberta wondered, to make him look like that? He looked—tormented. She soon found out.

'Of course I haven't got one of my women here!'

Roberta flinched, her whole body jerking in pained spasm. Of course, she thought grimly. I'm just a piece of nothing, not worth mentioning.

Quietly she climbed out of the bed, picked up her robe and shrugged it on.

'You know I love you, darling,' Mac stated heavily. 'But just for once can't you deal with this yourself?'

Whatever Lulu said then it was powerful enough to make Mac's shoulders sag in defeat. 'All right—all right!' he surrendered impatiently. 'If you really need me, then...'

His voice trailed off, the sound of the door opening behind him bringing him swinging around to face Roberta.

She paused, her gaze levelled on his impatient face. Go, she silently told him, and it will be the last time you'll ever get this close to me.

His eyes darkened, the tension in him so palpable that Roberta thought she could actually taste it. Then he lowered his dark gaze from her, thick lashes sweeping the passion out of his eyes as he said flatly, 'Yes. Of course I'll come. I'll catch the next flight out of here.'

And she turned away and walked out of the room.

Three days? she was thinking bitterly. He couldn't even give me one! Going over to the courtesy bar, she picked up a miniature bottle of French brandy, poured it into a glass, and swallowed it down in one fiery go.

'I'm sorry.' His voice came, quiet and protracted, from the bedroom doorway. Roberta turned to look at him. He was dressed again, looking as if he had never been out of those clothes tonight.

She turned away, the bitterness welling up inside her, too poisonous to give vent to.

'For goodness' sake, Roberta!' he rasped out harshly. 'I have no damned choice!'

'Choice? We all have choices, Mac,' she said flatly. 'And you've just made yours.'

'And that's it?' he bit out. 'Because you can't have all of me you want nothing at all? Doesn't that make you greedy, Roberta? Damned bloody selfish in fact?'

Did it? She supposed it did. 'In other words, unless I'm prepared to do all the compromising, I'm being selfish. Is that what you're saying?'

'No,' he sighed out heavily. 'I'm saying that the commitments that half rule my life are my problem to deal with as best as I can. But your insecurities about our relationship are your problem, sweetheart, to deal with the best *you* can.'

'My "insecurities", as you call them,' she flared up in derision, 'lie mostly in the fact that you still continue to deny my existence! Have you any idea how cheap and insignificant that makes me feel?'

Angry mockery scored across his face. 'So you would rather I told my distressed daughter to call back when I'm finished making love to you, would you?' he threw back scathingly.

'You had finished,' she reminded him. 'Then the phone started ringing, and you were back to denying I was even with you once again.'

'Oh, God,' he sighed, scoring a weary hand through his hair. 'I can't fight you on this one just now, Roberta. I have to go. Which doesn't mean I *want* to go!' he thrust out tightly at her bitter look. 'Only that I *have* to go! You have my complete loyalty in every way that is important to us, but I cannot pretend I have no family commitments just to ease your possessive streak. They're there. I have to deal with them. I can't offer you any more reassurance than that!'

And wasn't that right—how it should be? She censured her own resentfulness. Wouldn't she actually feel ashamed of him if he chose the other way? Of course his family had to come first. They were family! Flesh of his flesh! Just because her own family didn't have a nurturing gene between them, it did not mean she had the right to begrudge those who did!

'Then take me with you!' she pleaded impulsively, her face unknowingly vulnerable as she stared at him across the full width of the room. 'If you don't want to leave me, then take me with you! For goodness' sake, Mac!' she cried, when she saw the angry refusal already forming in his eyes. 'Give me something other than your body that says it's worth carrying this relationship on!'

He knew she meant it, too. There was a new light burning in her eyes that warned him that this time—this time she would not let him seduce her out of her resolve. It was up to him now to decide whether he was prepared to offer her more of himself than he had been doing or, more importantly perhaps, if he cared enough about her to offer her more.

'My God,' he sighed, flashing her a hard, impatient look, then, 'All right!' he surrendered. 'You can come!'

Her heart leapt, her chest expanding on a swell of triumph. 'Thank you,' she whispered shakily.

'Don't thank me, Roberta,' Mac answered grimly. 'I am doing this under protest, as you well know. You want more from me. You're getting more from me. But it's going to cause problems that I could well do without right now.'

He meant his family, and her leaping heart sank when she realised how much he resented her pushing him into a corner like this. But it was now or never, she reminded herself grimly. He might be right, and her timing was lousy, but would there ever be a right time for her to make a stand? Her experience to date said no, never—not while his family demanded more from him than possibly was fair.

Her chin came up, determination glowing in her green eyes to hold on to this bit of new ground she had won for herself, whether he liked it or not.

'And the Brunner deal?' she asked as calmly as she could. 'What do you want me to do about that, now we are both leaving Zurich?'

Mac paused as he was about to throw open the door, and she sensed a sudden tension in him before he turned back to glance at the file. 'Pack that,' he commanded.

'Joel won't be free to come here for a few more days so he can bring it back with him when he does.'

'And the calls?' she asked. 'Do you still want me to put through those calls to Brunner?'

'No.' He turned away again. 'Forget them. Forget the whole damned thing for now,' he decided impatiently. 'I'm going to find out the times of the London flights,' he said, then paused again, his gaze fixed on the still unopened door. 'Is this enough of the *more* you've been demanding from me?' he asked huskily.

Her chin came up, 'No,' she answered bravely. 'But it's a start.'

'As I said,' he sighed, 'you're a greedy woman, Roberta.'

'But still *your* woman,' she countered. 'As *you* like to claim.'

He made no reply to that one, but she saw his shoulders give a rueful shrug. 'See you later,' he said, then he was gone, leaving her to sink weakly into the nearest chair, feeling as though she had just run and won a marathon.

But he cared, she reminded herself staunchly. Three days—three whole days he had tried to put aside for her! And, even if Lulu's call had effectively ruined all of that, new hope began to flare like fire in her breast. Mac's family came first with him—perhaps they would always come first—but there was room in his heart for her too; she was sure of it now. And she was suddenly determined not to give up a single inch of that space without a damned good fight!

CHAPTER SEVEN

BY FIVE o'clock that same morning they were at the airport, waiting in the departure lounge for their flight to be called. The moment they'd checked in Mac had gone off to call the hospital to find out how Delia was.

Sitting waiting with their flight bags, Roberta watched him come striding back to her, the dark frown on his face filling her with a small sense of alarm.

'What's the matter?' she asked him sharply.

'I don't know,' he grunted, throwing himself down in the chair beside her. 'She's still in Theatre. For a straightforward appendix operation it seems to be taking an awful long time...'

'What time did they take her into Theatre?' Roberta asked concernedly.

He glanced at his watch. 'Almost four hours ago now.' He frowned again. 'I hope the bloody plane doesn't take off late!' he snapped, on a surge of anxious impatience.

Roberta reached out to touch his arm. 'She'll be all right,' she tried to assure him. 'Delia is fit and healthy. Whatever is complicating things she'll come through it all just fine.'

'It isn't Delia I'm worrying about,' he muttered, and got up, moving away on restless legs, leaving her to draw her own conclusions from that.

Lulu. He had to mean Lulu. Did that girl have any idea how lucky she was having a father like Mac? she wondered wistfully.

Arriving at Heathrow right in the middle of the commuter rush, Roberta blessed her own foresight in thinking of having a car laid on, ready and waiting to whip them into London. By then they were both tired; neither had slept. It had been gone two o'clock when Lulu's call had come through to Mac, and by the time they had packed and made arrangements to travel it had been almost time to leave for the airport to catch the first shuttle to London. Since leaving Zurich hardly a word had been exchanged between them. Mac had sunk deep into himself, waiting out the journey with a necessary patience, but the dark expression on his face had said that his concerned thoughts were with his daughter and his ex-wife and, wisely, Roberta had not tried to intrude.

It was mid-morning before they walked through the doors of the plush private hospital where Delia had been admitted. After a short conversation with the girl on Reception, who was unable—or unwilling—to tell them anything, they were directed towards the lifts and the floor that Delia's room was situated on.

It was evident as soon as the lift doors opened on to Lulu's strained white face that the poor child was almost frantic with worry.

She saw Roberta first, and for a moment something murderous snapped into the younger girl's eyes, then, as they stepped out of the lift, she was throwing herself into Mac's arms.

Mac caught her to him, his arms closing securely around this daughter who meant all the world to him. 'Oh, Daddy!' she cried. 'It's awful! Nobody will tell me anything, and she's been gone hours and hours!'

'Shush,' he murmured soothingly. 'Give me five minutes and I'll find out just what's been going on,' he assured her. 'Now, is there a waiting-room or some-thing, where you can wait while I——'

'I'm coming with you!' Lulu insisted tearfully. 'I want to see their faces when they try fobbing you off the same way they've been doing to me!'

Despite the gravity of the situation, Roberta couldn't help smiling at that. Like his daughter, she was well aware of Mac's intimidating force when he met with resistance in any way. Glancing at her over the top of Lulu's dark head, Mac saw the smile, and mocked it ruefully, taking a moment out himself to acknowledge the humour in the remark.

'Will you wait?' he then asked her huskily.

Roberta nodded. 'Don't worry about me,' she said. 'Just go and find out how Delia is.'

He nodded gratefully, then turned his attention back to Lulu, drawing the young girl beneath the crook of his shoulder and guiding her away.

Roberta watched them go, wishing she could be there with them, offering them both her support.

But she was quick to realise that there was a fine but definite line between support and intrusion. And one, she acknowledged as she went in search of the waiting-room, that she was going to have to learn to tread very carefully if Mac's family was ever going to accept her position in his life.

Not that treading that kind of line was anything new to her, she reminded herself grimly. Her whole life had been a series of fine lines drawn between herself and those people she cared about but who had other things in their lives which took precedence over her needs.

Like her parents, for instance, who were only ap-proachable as parents while between assignments. Then there was Aunt Sadie, who lived the obsessive life of a painter and, whenever she had found herself saddled with her young niece during school holidays, had managed to come up with just about anything to keep that child out of her hair so that her routine was not disturbed more than it needed to be. Aunt Sadie lived in a cottage quite close to Lake Windermere, which was perhaps fortunate for the middle-aged spinster, who didn't have much experience with children, because she had solved the problem by filling Roberta's time with just about any lakeland activity she could find for her! Sailing, skiing, windsurfing—— Wryly Roberta counted them off in her head. Outward-bound courses, rock-climbing, fell-walking—by the time she was eighteen, she'd become quite proficient in all of them! she recalled, with a smile that showed it hadn't all been horrible.

But it had been a different matter when she had been dumped on her two bachelor uncles, who had never taken their noses out of their stuffy books long enough to notice the lonely child that they'd been left in charge of. Experts on just about any classical subject you would like to mention, they lived for their fusty old books, and had expected her to be very quiet when around, so as not to disturb them. Those times had been perhaps some of the most miserable in her life, she remembered, recalling one particularly frightening day when she had taken ill with a rather nasty bout of tonsillitis that had knocked her completely flat. They hadn't known what to do with her! So they'd had her packed off to a private hospital where she'd stayed until it was time to go back to school.

She never went to them again after that. They said she broke their concentration. So, if Sadie wouldn't have her, she had stayed at school during the vacation breaks.

So maybe it wasn't surprising that, when it had come to choosing her own career, she'd gone for something about as far away from scholarly or artistic as she could get. She'd had enough of introvert people, and wanted to become a member of the real world. Where people interacted with each other on all levels. Where life was experienced at first hand—not through the second-hand media of books or an artist's palette or the lens of a camera. So she'd chosen business studies and joined the biggest company she could find once she'd graduated. Yet...

She frowned to herself. There had to be more of her family in her than she'd ever really considered before. Because, until Mac, and despite all the opportunities placed her way to be different, she had held herself aloof from most of them—treading warily instead of jumping into life with both feet as she had been so determined to do. Because restraint bred restraint—on an emotional level anyway, she acknowledged.

It had taken Mac and his dynamic personality to show her how to overthrow that restraint. And, even then, she had only ever done it for him.

The waiting-room door flew open. Roberta glanced up to find Lulu standing there, looking beautifully tragic with her jet-black hair tumbling in disarray about her slender shoulders. But it was her lovely blue eyes that held Roberta's attention. They had gone slightly wild with shock.

'Lulu!' Roberta gasped out in alarm. 'What's happened?'

'She's just come out of surgery! She looked awful! Tubes and bottles hanging all over the place! Daddy sent me in here while he finds out what he can. But...' She burst into tears.

'Oh, Lulu!' Roberta cried softly, jumping to her feet to take the poor girl in her arms.

It was a mark of just how badly Lulu was affected that she let Roberta hold her. She was trembling violently, the shock of seeing her mother like that having knocked her for six.

'Did they say why it had taken them so long?' she asked gently.

The silken dark head nodded against her shoulder. 'An ovarian cyst, wh-whatever that is,' she choked. 'It b-burst, and the p-poison w-went everywhere!' On another sob, the child shuddered at the horror of it. 'Th-they say she must have been feeling unwell for ages f-for it to get that bad. But she never so much as hinted at it! That's all your fault!'

Suddenly her head snapped up, and she gave Roberta a violent push, sending her staggering backwards while her blue eyes followed her with murder in them again.

'You!' she sliced at Roberta, before she'd even grasped hold of the first accusation. 'Turning up at my birthday party and flaunting your affair with Daddy!'

Flaunting! Roberta stared at her in stunned disbelief. 'Lulu,' she murmured soothingly, 'I would never——'

'You did—you did!' Lulu all but shrieked, not allowing Roberta to finish. 'You made Mummy so miserable that she didn't tell anyone she was feeling ill! Then y-you stalked out when Daddy wouldn't play up to you, and he s-snapped at everyone all weekend—including Mummy! He didn't even give her a lift back to London as he was supposed to do because he was too eager to get back to you!' The enmity in her eyes almost sliced Roberta in two. 'Th-then, when she did try to tell him she was ill, he'd gone chasing off to Zurich after you!

I hate you!' she cried. 'How can you live with yourself, coming between a man and his wife as you do?'

White-faced and trembling at the onslaught, Roberta blinked in astonishment at the last accusation. 'But your parents are no longer man and wife,' she said gently.

'Maybe not now,' Lulu conceded. 'But they will be again soon, if only you would go away!'

Roberta shook her head. 'You don't know what you're saying,' she said, accepting that shock was making the girl hysterical, even while she also accepted that the hatred coming from Lulu was real.

'Don't I?' Staring at her through hot, glinting eyes, Lulu's mouth turned down into an ugly sneer. 'They still sleep together, you know,' she announced. 'Every time Daddy comes to the house he goes to bed with Mummy.'

No. Roberta was not going to believe that. And neither was she going to argue with someone who was so obviously out of control. But the idea that Lulu could actually conjure up such an intimate scenario made her feel slightly sick, and she lowered her head so that Lulu wouldn't see her reaction on her face.

But she did see it, and completely misinterpreted it. 'Appals you, does it?' she taunted. 'The idea of my father going from your bed to hers? Well, what do you think it does to her? Why do you think she's always calling him up at that little love-nest he has set up for you—and why do you think he always comes running back to her? Because they still love each other, that's why,' she answered her own question. 'And one day they will get married again, whether you're still on the scene or not!'

'I think that's enough,' Roberta said quietly, lifting her white face to look coldly at the other girl. 'I accept that you're upset, and I accept that you're in shock. But if your father heard you talking like this he would be the appalled one.'

Lulu's eyes narrowed. 'You think I'm lying,' she said. 'But I'm not. How can you stay with a man like that?'

'I *know* you're lying,' Roberta corrected. 'I know your father has too much respect both for me and your mother to treat us as disgracefully as that. Don't you think,' she then suggested quietly, 'that you would be better putting all your energy into praying that your mother gets well, instead of using it up hating me?'

The younger girl blanched, the remark hitting home. But it didn't alter the depth of antipathy she was feeling towards Roberta. 'I'll get rid of you, out of our lives, if it's the very last thing I do!' she vowed.

Just then the door behind her opened and Mac walked in. On another flash of dark hostility, Lulu spun to face him, then threw herself, sobbing, into his arms. 'Oh, Daddy!' she sobbed. 'She's been saying the most horrible things to me! She says she hopes Mummy dies, and that when you marry her she'll make sure I never see you again!'

It was the raging of a deranged mind, and Roberta looked sadly at Mac, expecting him to acknowledge it, if only in a look. But as the moment stretched, with only Lulu's wretched sobbing to break the silence, an ice-cold sense of dread began to take her over.

No, she told herself with growing dismay. He couldn't possibly believe what Lulu had said.

'Send her away, Daddy!' Lulu sobbed. 'She hates me. Please send her away!'

Mac looked at Roberta over the top of Lulu's head. Tight-lipped and hard-eyed, he said, 'You'd better go.'

That was all, nothing else. And as she stood there, white-faced and staring at him, she could sense Lulu's triumphant laughter hiding behind those pretend tears.

'Mac. You——' At last she tried to defend herself, but it was too late, and he wasn't listening anyway. His attention was fixed firmly on his daughter, his arms and the soft sound of his voice all aimed to soothe her as he led her out of the door without a backward glance.

Roberta stared after them for a long, long time before it hit her, really hit her, what Mac had just done. Then, on realising it, she found she still could not move.

All right, she argued with herself. He had been in shock. Lulu had been in shock. Dear God, having listened to Lulu's garbled description of what had happened to her mother, they both had a right to be suffering from shock!

But it was what had come after Lulu had told her about Delia that was holding her stiff and still. All that bitter bile that had spewed from Lulu's mouth—the hatred and resentment that had been all too real. Then the quick-thinking lies she had flung at her father in an effort to show Roberta in a bad light.

And Mac's face. She shuddered. The expression on his face had been all too real also. He had looked at Roberta with a cold contempt that had frozen the blood in her veins.

She didn't for one moment doubt that Mac would see Lulu's lies for exactly what they were once he'd had time to think about them. But could she live with that depth of hatred and resentment constantly coming between herself and Mac?

No. She looked down to where her hands were still trembling in reaction to Lulu's vicious onslaught, and knew she could not continue to take that kind of treatment on the chin, with no right to retaliate. Her own pride would not allow her to.

And as long as Mac continued to refuse her the weapons to retaliate there was no hope for them as a couple.

Choices. They were back to choices, and Mac had once again made his. And, with shock as an excuse or not, she accepted now that the balance would always be tipped Lulu's way.

Mac didn't love Roberta, but he loved his daughter. Blood was thicker than water. Sex was no substitute for love. She could never compete with that, and it was way past time that she accepted that.

She had to get away, she realised, on a sudden burst of movement that sent her walking stiffly to the door. And not only from this hospital, but from everything— Mac, work, the lot.

She needed to be alone to think, think long and hard about what she was going to do with her life.

She needed to go home...

And where was that? she asked herself bleakly as she stepped inside the waiting lift. There was a place in Oxfordshire that she supposed could be called home. She had a key to the front door of the red-bricked detached house, and a room upstairs that she supposed she could call her own, though she had spent very little time in it. Her parents wouldn't be there because they rarely ever were.

But at least she could virtually guarantee her own solitude while she came to some decisions about herself.

The idea was tempting, so tempting, in fact, that by the time a taxi had dropped her off at Jenny's flat she had her next few hours firmly planned out.

Jenny was still at work—for which Roberta was grateful, because it saved her having to explain why she was back so early from Zurich and why she was quickly repacking her suitcase with fresh clothes before shooting off again.

Instead she left Jenny a note that just said simply, 'Gone away for a few days. See you when I get back.' Then, armed with her fresh clothes, the keys to her rarely used car and the keys to her parents' house, she left for Oxfordshire, stopping only once on the way to pick up the necessary provisions to see her through the next few days.

As she expected the house was empty, lacking the warmth that came naturally to a place where people were actually living. It was clean, though, neat and tidy, because her parents employed a lady who came in a couple of times a week to keep it that way.

Dropping her suitcase down in the hall, she went back to the car to collect her bags of shopping, efficiently storing them all away in the right places before making a third trip outside to garage the car so that no over-zealous neighbour would come snooping around to see who was using the Chandler house while they were away.

A few minutes after that and the coffee-pot was full to the brim with freshly ground, invitingly scented coffee, and she sat down at the kitchen table with it—to wilt, rather like a flower when it was starved of oxygen.

Or like a human being when starved of any more excuses to keep depression at bay.

Grimacing at the miserable thought, she poured steaming coffee into her cup, then just sat staring grimly down at it.

It was late in the afternoon, and the September sun had already dropped so low in the sky that dusk was

beginning to draw in. Outside there was no wind, nothing
to disturb the mood of darkening depression beginning
steadily to close her in. This was rural Oxfordshire, and
the nearest house to here was at least half a mile away.
The lane that ran alongside the house was used only by
the few houses dotted along its five-mile length.

So the silence was total—a luxury she had not experienced in a long time, London being the noisy, busy
city it was.

It was strange, really, but just like the last time she'd
reached this same milestone in her relationship with Mac.
She felt calm, superbly composed, refusing to let anything even vaguely upsetting creep into her mind.

She was tired, she recognised that. Physically
exhausted by lack of sleep and emotionally exhausted
by too many battles with Mac.

So she sat on and on, not drinking the waiting coffee
or even thinking much, but just letting the increasing
darkness and a sense of complete aloneness in the world
slowly close her in.

Maybe she dozed off. She could have done, though
she wasn't absolutely sure. But a sudden noise brought
her jerking out of her odd half-awareness, just in time
for the kitchen door to fly open and the light to flick
blindingly on.

She blinked, then didn't do anything else but sit there,
staring at the two people standing staring back at her
from the doorway.

Her hair was long, sun-bleached to a near whiteness,
the ends so in need of professional attention that they
stuck out like straw from a tied bale. And her face was
tanned to the point that it had taken on the properties
of old leather. She was wearing jeans, jeans so old and
tatty that a tramp would turn his nose up at them, and

her yellow-coloured sweatshirt looked as if it had been
slept in for days.

He looked no better. His straggly red hair and beard
almost obliterated his face. His clothes—an exact match
to hers—hung on a body that was so tall and thin, it
looked as though the slightest puff of wind would knock
it over. But that was a fallacy, because that body was
built of high-tensile wire, and so full of restless energy
that even while he stood there so very still his eyes were
alive. Green—bright green—with shock, surprise and a
lot of consternation.

Her parents, Roberta thought wryly. In their fifties,
yet they looked like a pair of hippy teenagers who had
just hitch-hiked back from some wild rock concert. And
the consternation that they were too shocked to hide was
just how teenagers would feel if they walked in to find
a stern parent waiting to give them a dressing-down.

They never had known how to respond to her—this
child they had farmed out as much as they possibly
could, and sent away to boarding-school as soon as they
possibly could. This child who, because of her unusual
upbringing, had grown into a coolly beautiful, very
sophisticated young woman who was so many light-years
away from what they were themselves that she was a
stranger to them. A phenomenon they did not
understand.

'Bobby!' her father gasped, being the first to find his
voice. 'What are you doing here?'

Bobby. Roberta smiled and wryly shook her head.
Bobby! He'd called her that when she was one year old.
Called her that when she was ten. Still called her that
when she was fifteen and had begged him not to, because it sounded so boyish to a girl who so desperately
wanted to be a woman.

He had called her that only a couple of weeks ago, when she'd rung up in the vague hope of catching them between assignments. 'Hi, Bobby, what do you want?' he'd asked, making her feel as though she only called them up when she wanted something—which was grossly untrue.

'To see you both, with a bit of luck,' she'd therefore thrown back drily, putting him immediately on the defensive.

'But we're off to Africa tomorrow,' he'd complained. 'Barely got time to turn around. Will it wait until we get back?'

Would *it* wait. Not would *she* wait. She'd felt like a dog left at the local kennels—a fluffy white West Highland called Bobby, left to pine for the return of its owners. Had always felt a bit like that.

What was it with these two that they could never seem to see her as anything more important to them than a little pet dog? In fact she had a horrible idea that they would love a pet dog more!

Would *know* how to love a dog more.

God, if she couldn't see that she had her father's green eyes and her mother's blonde hair, she would have wondered long ago if the hospital had mixed two babies up on the day she was born! Hell! Maybe there was a blonde-haired green-eyed twenty-five-year-old hippy running about somewhere, with a camera dangling around her neck and an unquenchable urge to study anything on four legs!

She began to laugh, the idea suddenly striking her as very funny, because it brought on another scenario, where she could see two very conservative people struggling to bring up their wayward daughter who found more pleasure in studying the mating habits of mice than

wearing pretty dresses and learning to dance and play
the piano.

A cuckoo in their nest.

Was she a cuckoo in the nest?

Through eyes swimming with laughter she looked at
them, saw her mother's leathery face and her father's
fuzzy red one. Then she thought about those other two
fictitious parents she had just conjured up—staunch,
conservative, upright members of the community.

And suddenly she wasn't laughing. She was crying.
Sobbing as though her heart would break because,
whatever these two outrageous people were to her, she
loved them! She loved them so very much that it didn't
matter who they were or what they were—or even *if* they
were!

She loved them, and she wished she knew how to tell
them that, because she needed their support right now.
Needed to know that they loved her.

Her tears had further surprised them; she could feel
that in the sudden increase in tension in the room. She
rarely cried, couldn't remember the last time she had
broken down in front of them. But now she had started
she couldn't seem to stop, and as her sobbing went on
and on from somewhere near by she heard the sound of
shuffling feet, of plastic knocking against metal, and
voices gasping in alarm. Then an arm came warmly
around her shoulders, and someone else was grabbing
at her hands.

Parents. One to hug her and feel secure with, and one
to tell all her wretched problems to.

A bit of what Lulu Maclaine had a lot of.

'Roberta, sweetheart—whatever is the matter?' her
mother murmured concernedly.

That seemed to do it—for the first time in her life her mother was sounding genuinely concerned for her, and it opened more floodgates, from where words came flowing out. She could barely believe she was doing it! But she told them everything.

She told them about Mac and her love for him, about his family and his love for them. She told them about Lulu's party and what came after. She told them about Zurich and what came after that. She even told them about themselves, and what she thought of them. And it was only when the tears and the words had been drained right out of her that she realised with dawning embarrassment that they had listened to it all without offering a single word themselves.

'I came down here to be alone—to think,' she heard herself explain defensively, her heart heavy because she knew they didn't know what to say to her. 'I—I didn't expect you to be here.'

'Why should you?' her mother said with grim irony. 'We've never been here for you before, so why should you expect it of us now?'

'I didn't mean that,' Roberta said uncomfortably. 'I meant——'

'I know what you meant, Roberta,' her mother cut in drily. 'But I know what I meant too...'

A short silence fell, filled with nervous tension brought on by her mother's unexpected remark and Roberta's inability to respond to it. Then her father cleared his throat.

'Er—you haven't asked us what we're doing here,' he prompted huskily.

'Oh!' Roberta's watery eyes widened at the reminder. 'I thought you two were in Africa?'

'We were, only...' Pulling out a chair, he sat down, then casually began to tell her about warring factions and political unrest and confiscated visas. It might not be the most demonstrative way of soothing an emotional daughter down but by the time he got to the part where they ended up flying back out having never left the airport or used a single reel of film she was feeling much calmer, and was able to listen with real if rueful enjoyment to his version of a comedy of disasters. 'Hence the filthy clothes,' he concluded wryly. 'And the definite unkempt and unhygienic look about us. They wouldn't even let us have our luggage so we could change!'

'So.' Her mother took up the story as she came to sit down with a fresh pot of steaming coffee. 'Having had to put the whole damned project on the shelf for now, we decided to come straight home, bath and generally make ourselves respectable, then try to book ourselves a holiday. You know, somewhere normal like Majorca or Tenerife. And have the real break we've been promising ourselves for years now.'

'Sounds great,' Roberta murmured wistfully, wishing she could just take off for two whole weeks to do nothing but eat, sleep and swim—and forget all her problems for a while. But she'd already had her quota of holiday weeks for this year. She had taken them while Mac was in the Caribbean with Lulu, she remembered heavily. She and Jenny had gone off to Italy, doing the sights in Florence and Rome.

'Come with us,' her mother invited impulsively. 'If you're feeling this low, darling, it would do you good to have a complete break.'

'I'm sorry,' she refused. 'But I can't.' And she was genuinely regretful. 'I'm pinching time off work by being here now. If I'm not back at my desk by Monday, the company would have every right to dock my pay.'

'Don't you think you've earned the right to take a couple of extra weeks off from Maclaines?' her father said harshly.

'Joshua!' her mother gasped as Roberta went pale, the sharp thrust of that remark hitting well and truly home.

'Well!' he muttered angrily. 'I may be better at understanding the habits of wild animals, but that doesn't mean I don't recognise it when a man is using a woman for his own convenience!'

'You're right,' Roberta agreed, as always ruthlessly honest about herself. And it was that same honesty that forced her to add, 'But he used me only because I let myself be used.' Her chin came up, green eyes defying her father to dispute that point.

He couldn't, and it was he who dropped his gaze first.

Just then the phone began to ring, sending all three of them still. Her father glanced questioningly at her. 'Could it be for you?' he asked.

'Maybe.' Roberta shrugged. 'I didn't tell anyone where I was going but...' It might be Mac, she thought dully. It might be Jenny looking for her. But...

'Do you want to talk to them?'

'No, she doesn't,' her mother answered for her. 'She doesn't wish to talk to anyone for the next few days.'

Glancing up sharply, she caught the tail-end of a look being exchanged between her mother and father. Whatever it meant, her father nodded grimly, then walked away.

'Well?' her mother challenged. 'You don't want to speak to anyone, do you?'

'No,' she answered huskily.

'Then you won't have to.' With a short pat on
Roberta's shoulder she got up, then paused to look down
on her grimly. 'We may have been rotten parents to you,
Roberta,' she said, 'but we do love you. And for once
we're going to stay around long enough to prove it—
even if that means staying here in Oxford rather than
jetting off on holiday.'

'But I can't let you do that!' Roberta cried, not seeing
the little trap her mother was coolly setting her. 'It would
make me feel as guilty as sin if you did!'

Her father came back. Roberta looked at him with
helpless expectation glowing in her eyes.

'It was for me, not you,' he murmured apologetically,
and grimly watched the life fade out of her again.

'Our plans have changed,' her mother informed him
coolly. 'We're not going abroad. We're going to stay here
to be close to Roberta instead.'

'No, you're not,' Roberta put in. 'I'll come,' she said
dully. 'I'll come with you. I'll come.'

But whether she had changed her mind in sharp disappointment because the phone call had not been Mac
trying to find her or whether she had because she was
suffering from shock at her parents' caring attitude
Roberta didn't know.

CHAPTER EIGHT

WHICHEVER, it turned out to be the best decision she had made in a long time. Not only did two weeks of complete relaxation help her to get her head and her heart sorted out, but they also gave her time to get to know her mother and father. And the more she came to know them, the more she came to understand just what it was that drove them as hard as it did.

They talked passionately about world pollution and the ecological balance, and how animal life quality was the barometer of human life quality. And of how they tried to get these points across via their documentaries. They described to her how much time and patience it took to follow a particular species through a complete cycle of its life, to monitor, log on film its interaction with others of its species, and what it had to do just to survive.

Just walking the seashore with them was an experience in itself, for they could pick up a single shell and give a knowledgeable narration on what it was, where it came from and why it was now lying on this particular beach.

But sometimes, as they talked and showed her things, she felt like a child again—a child who should have been shown these wonders at five or seven or nine years old, not at twenty-five. And, as if they too had become aware of the same, they would suddenly change the subject and talk of other things—force her to talk about herself until the awkward moment had gone again.

Yet these moments also drew them closer together. Roberta recognised that she would never become a full disciple of their fascinating life. Too much time had gone by for her to change what circumstances had moulded her into. And there were too many memories of feeling lost and cast out while they chased their personal rainbows for her ever to completely forgive them their neglect of her. But at least she learned to understand them, and maybe even admire them for their total dedication.

By the time she arrived back in London she was feeling much calmer emotionally too. Long hours spent lying on a beach, with nothing else to do but think, had helped her pull her life back into perspective.

She loved Mac. That was an unalterable fact. But she had also come to accept that a one-sided love could not sustain a relationship and sustain an acceptable amount of self-esteem at the same time.

She needed to break completely free from the Maclaine power, and the only way to do that was to leave the company, find herself another job and try to start afresh without the constant pull on her emotions that the Maclaine name automatically had.

So it was with that decision fixed firmly in her mind that she walked into the Maclaine building two weeks later.

The first person she saw was Mitzy. 'Wow, don't you look fantastic!' she said, eyeing Roberta's carefully nurtured golden tan and the flattering effect it had on her lovely green eyes and pale blonde hair. 'And are you in deep trouble!' she then added sagely.

Roberta smiled at the compliment and peaked a pale eyebrow at the warning. It was Mitzy she had spoken to before she'd gone off to Spain, leaving the poor secretary to break the news to Joel that his assistant was taking an unscheduled two weeks off without permission.

'I don't know what's been going on since you did a bunk,' Mitzy said, 'but all hell has been let loose in here. The Big Mac has had one hell of a bust-up with the Little Mac. He was heard blasting at him with enough heat to solder his feet to the ground,' she informed Roberta drily. 'It seemed to revolve around the fact that you had been allowed to disappear off the face of the earth, and what the hell did Joel think he was doing letting it happen! To which Joel demanded what the hell did he expect you to do—wait around until he had time for pillow-talk again? Which,' Mitzy said drolly at Roberta's stiffening look, 'took the top right off the Big Mac's temper, I can tell you. Since then he's been stomping around like a giant with big boots on—you know?' she prompted. 'Thundering and lightning all over the place?'

'And how do you know all of this?' Roberta coolly enquired.

'Because I listened,' Mitzy admitted. 'With my ear to that door over there.' She pointed to Joel's closed office door. 'I got the impression that most of it was over the Brunner deal, but——' she shrugged her disappointment '—couldn't quite catch enough to be sure. What did happen out there in Zurich?' she then asked Roberta curiously.

'Nothing,' she answered, then asked, for her own curiosity, 'How did the Brunner deal finish in the end?'

'Oh.' Mitzy's eyes went wide again. 'Didn't you know? The Big Mac settled all of that before he left Zurich!'

Roberta frowned. 'But he couldn't have done,' she protested. 'He hadn't even had any contact with Franc Brunner before he left!'

Mitzy just shrugged all that away. 'Well, I have a copy
of the whole deal around here somewhere,' she said, beginning to hunt through the mounds of paperwork clut-
tering her desk. 'Yes!' she cried. 'Here it is!' She handed
it to Roberta. 'See—Big Mac's signature on the bottom
next to Brunner's. And the date,' she prompted, 'look
at the date. He closed it out the same day you both arrived in Zurich. You've got to give it to the guy,' she
sighed admiringly, 'nothing stops him once he's been
wound up! And look at the price they eventually settled
on!' She then added for good measure, 'We'd shot way
past that weeks before he came in on it!'

Roberta was looking. She was thinking too. Thinking
things that made her blood begin to simmer and sent
two weeks' hard-won serenity shooting right out of her
head.

'Where's Joel?' she demanded tightly, pulling off her
coat to reveal a black dress beneath that did the most
amazing things to her figure.

'In his office,' Mitzy said, frowning at the plain white
envelope Roberta produced before discarding her bag
along with her coat. 'But if you've got any sense,
Roberta,' she warned as Roberta went striding towards
Joel's closed office door, 'you'll go upstairs before seeing
Joel! Only, the Big Mac has already rung down here,
demanding to see you, and it's only five past nine now!'

'Blow Mac,' she muttered. 'I'll go and see him when
I'm good and ready!'

Joel's door swung open. He was sitting at his desk,
looking grim-faced and fed up. But he brightened when
he saw her. 'Roberta!' he cried, coming to his feet. 'You
look great! The break has obviously done you good!'

'It had,' she agreed, walking briskly to his desk. 'Until
I came back here and saw this!' Angrily she slapped the

copy of the Brunner deal down in front of him. 'What does all this mean, Joel?' she demanded.

'Mean?' He looked uncomfortable all of a sudden. 'It means Mac clinched us a damned good deal—what the heck do you think it means?' he asked offhandedly. 'I don't know why you're glaring at me like that, Roberta,' he snapped. 'You knew Mac had gone out there to sort it all out!'

'Yes,' she agreed. 'But I hadn't realised how *quickly* he'd sorted it all out,' she explained. 'Like by the end of the very same day he arrived!'

'Oh.' Joel sat down again. 'Didn't he tell you? That would be the emergency with Delia getting in the way,' he decided with a smile.

'Or more likely because he didn't want me to know he had sorted it out at all!' she snapped. 'What kind of game were you and your brother playing with me, Joel?' she demanded to know. 'Was I sent out to Zurich for no other reason than that Mac wanted me there?'

He flushed, an answer in itself. More confirmation came when he turned defensive. 'Look,' he said uncomfortably, 'don't spit at me—spit at my brother! He's the one who set you up!'

'With your help!' she snapped. 'Which makes me all the more certain that I am doing the right thing in giving you this!' And she held the plain white envelope out towards him.

Joel looked at it, and instantly recognised it for exactly what it was. 'I can't accept it,' he refused, shaking his head.

'You can,' Roberta countered smoothly. 'Because I insist.' Pointedly she put the envelope down on the desk between them.

'Oh, hell, Roberta,' he sighed heavily. 'Don't do this to me! He'll skin me alive if you do!'

'I tell you what, Joel,' she suggested softly, 'while he's skinning you alive, you skin him. Then it will be just like old times, won't it? One brother using the other brother to get what he wants?'

'I can't help it if he pulled rank on me over the Brunner thing!' he sighed. 'Take issue with him, if you need to take issue with anyone! He's the one who really counts, after all!'

'Oh, I mean to take issue with him,' Roberta assured him. 'But just tell me one more thing before I do,' she asked. 'Was Karl Loring a set-up too? Mac said you'd realised he was trying to pull a fast one over you, yet you still had him meet me when I arrived.'

He had the grace to flush. 'I thought a bit of competition might help bring Mac to his senses about you,' he admitted grudgingly.

Oh, it had, Roberta acknowledged silently. It had activated his possessive streak long enough for him to stake his claim on her again. But it had only lasted as long as it took his daughter to restake *her* claim on *him*.

'How is Delia, by the way?' she enquired as an aside.

Joel looked up and grimaced. 'Not bad now,' he said. 'Went through the mill a bit at the time. They had to pump her full of antibiotics to kill the spread of infection and she's lucky to be still alive, to tell the truth. Still——' he shrugged '—she's getting over it and should be coming home in a few days. Roberta,' he then pleaded, 'take back this letter—at least until you've spoken to Mac!'

'No,' she refused. 'I don't like being used, Joel,' she told him tightly. 'And between you and your brother you've been using me for just about every purpose you can think of!'

'Where are you going?' he demanded when she turned to leave.

'To take issue with the boss, as you suggested I do,' she answered tartly.

'Then at least take this with you!' he said, lurching forward to pick up the envelope and pushing it at her. 'If you're going to resign to anyone, then do it to him. I'm not brave enough to accept it!'

She took the envelope and walked out, well aware that Joel didn't think she would end up going through with it. She would, though, she vowed. She was more determined than ever to get away from Mac's influence now!

She was still coldly furious when she walked into Mac's office without knocking a few minutes later.

He was standing at the window, staring out at the bird's-eye view he had of London. He wasn't wearing a jacket and his hands were lost inside the pockets of his beautifully tailored dark grey trousers. Roberta felt the usual sensation of hot breathlessness attack her, as it usually did when she first set eyes on him, but firmly squashed the feeling with contempt.

She wasn't here to drool over him. She was here to——

'Where the hell have you been?' Mac bit out furiously, turning on her like a dog preparing to bite.

She blinked, his sudden angry snarl having taken the initiative right away from her.

But only for a moment. 'Away!' she said. 'Abroad—to get away from you!'

His eyes glinted at her simmering contempt. 'This is not your ex-lover talking to you, Miss Chandler, it's your chairman, demanding a full explanation from you!'

Ex-lover? Roberta went pale. It was the first time Mac had ever used that prefix to her, and it hit her so hard that she almost gasped in pain.

'Now,' he prompted tightly, when he saw that he had made his point, 'where have you been?'

'S-Spain,' she answered, hating that tell-tale little stammer that crept into her voice. 'Majorca, to be exact. My parents have friends who have a villa there. They let us use——'

'Your parents?' he cut in incredulously. 'You went away with your parents?'

'I do possess parents, you know!' she said stiffly, offended by his tone.

'Yes,' he jeered. 'Parents you always professed to hate!'

'I never said I hated my parents!' she protested.

Mac pulled an irritable face. 'Loved them, but held them in contempt, then,' he amended shortly, adding deridingly, 'You know, like you do me!'

'I've never said that either!' she denied. 'We just—never understood each other very well, that's all. But now we do.'

'Who—me? Or your parents?' he mocked.

'My parents!' she snapped. 'I'll never in a million years come to understand you! And will you please tell me if I am still having this conversation with my boss?' she then demanded impatiently. 'Because it naturally makes a difference to how I reply!'

Mac sighed and scraped an angry hand through his hair. 'How the hell should I know?' he muttered. 'I'm just one person to everyone else; it's only with you that I seem to become two.'

'Then that should teach you to keep your hands off the paid staff, shouldn't it?' she mocked, regaining her self-confidence and her anger as his died away. 'Which reminds me,' she added, her chin coming up to challenge him. 'Zurich,' she said. 'And the so-called Brunner deal?'

'Ah.' He glanced at her thoughtfully, and saw in her accusing eyes that she knew the truth. 'I'm not going to apologise to you, Roberta,' he said ruefully. 'So you may as well drop the frozen doll act.'

'So you did have me sent to Zurich for your own purposes!' she gasped.

His black brows rose at her way of putting it. 'I had you sent to Zurich,' he responded, 'to give us some time alone together to try to resolve our problems.'

'You mean to try to get me back in your bed!' she corrected him bitterly.

His dark eyes hardened at that. 'Oh, of course!' he agreed sardonically. 'What other possible reason could I have for plotting to get you alone there if it wasn't to get you into my bed?'

'My God, Mac!' she breathed shakily. 'You're a devious swine!'

'True.' His curt nod acknowledged it, but then he added with withering sarcasm, 'But what a waste of time and effort it turned out to be, when all it took was one concerted attack on your supposedly determined sense to have you falling straight into bed with me! Which makes you—what, exactly?' he hit back ruthlessly.

Easy, she thought, lowering her eyes to hide the shame evident in their depths. 'How did you do it?' she whispered thickly. 'How did you close that Brunner deal so quickly?'

He shrugged, his whole demeanour arrogantly dismissive. 'My arrangements to meet with Brunner were sorted out before I even left London,' he informed her.

'We talked, and exchanged contracts over dinner—while you kindly kept Loring busy by letting him seduce you over the red wine!'

Her chin came up at his deriding choice of words. But as for the rest, it fell neatly into place. Just the mere mention to Brunner that the great Solomon Maclaine was taking over the deal must have been enough to make him grovel in panic. Just as the same name had made Karl Loring rush out in panic, she remembered bitterly. Eager to make his warning phone calls to Brunner, only to discover, no doubt, that Karl himself had been sold down the line!

A bit like she had herself—which reminded her, and, walking stiffly forward, she laid the white envelope on his desk. 'Joel was too frightened of you to accept this, so I'm giving it to you myself. My resignation,' she explained.

Mac stared at it, then at her. 'Is this another of your sweet ways of telling me we're finished?' he questioned cynically.

'There was never anything to finish,' she returned. 'As you've just taken great pains to explain to me, I was there to be used, and easy in the process.'

Mac let out a heavy sigh. 'You know I didn't mean a single word of it,' he said. 'I was being nasty—telling you what you like to believe! Hasn't it ever occurred to you, Roberta, that it isn't *me* who has a low opinion of you, but you who has one of yourself?'

She looked down and away. Perhaps he was right. But it wasn't his opinion or even her own that had beaten her in the end. It was his daughter's.

'My resignation stands, Mac,' she inserted firmly.

'Not while I'm around to block it, it doesn't,' he countered.

Refusing to take any notice, she turned away.

'Don't you damned well dare,' he bit our threaten- ingly, bringing her determined stride to a halt. 'You've walked out on me once too often already, Roberta. This time you see the fight through to the end.'

'And what are we fighting about this time, Mac?' she demanded as she spun back. 'My leaving your company or my leaving you? Only, I'd really like to know, be- cause I've lost the thread of this one!'

'Both!' he snapped. 'Neither! Since you aren't going to do either!' Grimly he came towards her. 'Two bloody weeks I've waited to have this out with you!' he growled when he reached her. 'Two weeks! And what do you do? You calmly walk in here with your resignation all typed out and a look of outraged indignation on your face!' His hands gripped her shoulders and gave her a shake. 'What is it with you, Roberta, that I feel as if no sooner have I taken one step forward than I'm taking two steps back?'

'Explain what the step forward is towards and I'll answer the question,' she countered tartly.

His eyes darkened, the look beginning to burn in them one she knew of old. 'You!' he muttered. 'They're always towards you, you fool! Why can't you see that?'

'Because a huge great obelisk called "family" stands in the way, that's why!' she snapped, and watched him as he gave a short, weary sigh.

'I'm sorry,' he said tightly, 'for what happened at the hospital.'

'I thought you said you weren't going to apologise to me,' she reminded him, her chin back up again, eyes coolly challenging.

'Not for the Brunner thing,' he agreed. 'But I will for Lulu. You have to understand,' he said heavily. 'She's so damned volatile—highly strung! And——'

And selfish, and spoiled, and possessed of a dangerous tongue, Roberta thought, but kept those thoughts to herself.

'And she'd just suffered a terrible shock,' he went on. 'It made her feel frightened—insecure! So she said some very wild things to you that she quickly regretted later.'

'Good,' Roberta said. 'I'm glad she realised her mistake.' Or tactical error, to put it more honestly. Like Roberta, Lulu had obviously realised that her father was not so stupid as to believe those awful things she'd said.

'For God's sake!' he rasped, seeing something in her face that must have let him know she was being sarcastic, even if her voice hadn't shown it. 'Her mother was ill—almost dying in front of her eyes!' He gave her another frustrated shake. 'Can't you show a little compassion and feel something less than enmity towards her?'

Could she? Roberta wondered. Perhaps she could— if Lulu ever showed something less than enmity towards herself.

And that was like tossing your cap at rainbows, she mocked herself cynically.

'Will you endorse my resignation,' she parried, 'if I do?'

'No,' he growled, 'I will not.' His mouth tightened at her continuing caustic manner. 'But I'm damned well happy to do—this!'

He was so quick that she didn't even see him move! But suddenly—as always!—she found herself back in his arms, with his mouth covering hers, and he was kissing her with a hunger that took every ounce of strength she had in her to fight.

'Open your mouth,' he commanded when she held her lips tightly shut. She shook her head, refusing to comply. 'I can make you,' he warned. 'I only have to do this.' And he bit sensuously down on her bottom lip, drawing the tender fullness into his mouth and sucking delicately on it. 'Now the teeth,' he instructed, when her mouth eventually parted on a wretched gasp. His tongue traced the clean white front of her tightly clenched teeth, sliding against the sensitive inner tissue of her mouth as it did so. 'Give in, Roberta,' he urged, when she began to tremble at the effort it cost her not to. 'You know you want to.'

No, I don't, she thought bleakly. But I can't seem to help myself. And she felt a shudder of pleasure ripple through her as his hands ran caressingly down her sides to clasp her hips. That action forced her own hands to lift, to maintain her balance; her fingers clutched at the fine cotton of his shirt, then, because they couldn't resist it, spread greedily over the hard-muscled warmth of the body beneath.

He groaned in pleasure at her touch, then moved against her—not aroused, but getting there. The heat coming from him and the pulsing rhythm worked like a drug on her own desire. On a soft, defeated sigh, her teeth parted—but just to punish him for doing this to her again she bit down hard on the tip of his tongue before surrendering completely.

Instead of protesting at her little bit of cannibalism he laughed, the sound husky with mocking triumph. 'You little minx,' he murmured, then, to pay her back, gripped the back of her neck and forced her head right back so that he could bear down on her mouth with an assault that drained her right through to her very core.

The phone on his desk began to ring. For a few hectic moments neither of them seemed to hear it. Then the sound impinged on Roberta's mind and she dragged her mouth away from his.

'Answer the phone,' she whispered.

He ignored it. 'You know, your eyes go the most incredible shade of green when you're aroused,' he remarked instead, keeping her face tipped up to him. 'It's a kind of ocean-green colour that makes me want to dive straight in.'

'That's corny,' she derided, not in the least impressed. 'Answer the phone.' It was still ringing away persistently. 'You're better at that. You never know,' she taunted provokingly, 'it may be important—like Delia needing a bunch of grapes, or Lulu wanting to check you haven't got a woman here.'

The hand at her neck tightened. His eyes—a dusky shade of slumberous grey when aroused—snapped into a gun-metal hardness. 'For such a beautiful woman you have a vicious little tongue in your head!' he said harshly.

'Don't I just,' she agreed, and provoked him even further by pressing the said tongue out between falsely smiling teeth. Inviting him to bite back.

He might be able to beat her easily with his damned sex appeal, but it wasn't all one-sided. Mac had never been able to resist her when she teased him like this.

He must have been thinking the same thing, because he suddenly relaxed again. 'You know how to press all the right buttons, don't you?' he sighed, then swooped, covering that inviting bit of tongue with his at the same time as his mouth closed sensuously over her own.

The phone didn't stop. But neither did the kiss. So both went on and on, one seeming to compete with the other until, on a frustrated growl, Mac gave up the battle and, still keeping a hold on her, took the few steps back to his desk to snatch up the receiver.

'What?' he barked.

Roberta smiled, and was glad it wasn't her on the other end of the line.

'Oh,' he then said disconcertedly, 'Jenson. Thanks for returning my call.' He let go of Roberta to swing a hip onto the desk, giving her a chance to move a couple of desperately needed paces away. 'No—no,' he assured the caller. 'You weren't interrupting anything. Just a problem employee.' His mocking eyes clashed with Roberta's, then dipped lazily over her long, slender body. 'I've thoroughly dealt with her now,' he said.

Her green eyes flashed, his grey ones challenged. Whatever the man called Jenson was saying to him was doing nothing to intrude on an eye-to-eye battle that was so sexually rooted that Roberta could feel her senses responding like well-tuned chords to a musician's hands.

'Great,' he said suddenly, breaking the spell. 'It's all set up, then. I'll be catching the afternoon flight out of Heathrow and will be with you by——' he glanced at his watch '—two o'clock your time.'

Your time? Afternoon flight? Roberta went still, quickly trying to work out just what all that could mean. Then her heart made a sinking dive, because she suddenly recognised the name Jenson, and that could only mean New York.

Mac was flying out to New York this afternoon, to consult with his head of enterprises over there, and once again she was being left alone and frustrated, half made love to and half defeated by a man who played around with her feelings as if they were inanimate toys!

'I like the dress,' he murmured, making her aware that he had finished his call and was now eyeing the simple black wool dress she was wearing, which hugged her figure from throat to wrist to knee. 'It makes me want to peel it off you. Is the gorgeous tan all over—or are those interestingly intimate bits still creamy white?'

'None of your business,' she snapped, trying to come to terms with this latest in a long line of mood-flatteners that Mac was so good at dealing out.

'I could take you, right here across this desk,' he murmured, 'and simply find out for myself.'

'Sorry,' she refused. 'But that's one delight I'm saving for the man I marry.'

'Ah,' he said, again showing that he was never slow on the uptake. 'We're back to fighting again, are we?' On a grimace, he turned a little so that both hips rested on the desk, then folded his arms across his chest. 'What caused it this time?' he asked wearily.

She ignored that. 'I've offered you my resignation,' she reminded him. 'I'm still waiting for you to endorse it.'

He ignored *that.* 'Meet someone while you were on holiday, did you?'

'What if I did?' she challenged. 'It is my sole aim in life to find a man who really understands and respects what a woman like me needs,' she informed him coolly.

He had the cheek to laugh at that. 'I understand you very well when you've got your legs wrapped around me and I'm lost deep inside you,' he stated teasingly. 'And I entirely respect your need to have me that way sometimes!'

'Sex!' she sighed in disgust. 'You always have to bring everything down to sex!'

'Great sex,' he extended. 'Mind-blowing, totally-out-of-ourselves sex! Does this guy who's to have the privilege of taking you across my desk give you anything even remotely as good as that?'

Roberta stared at him for a moment in complete bewilderment. 'You're crazy—do you know that?' she gasped. 'Having a conversation with you is like walking through a maze! There's never any beginning to it or a proper end!'

'And with you it's like treading carefully through a minefield of contrariness!' he threw right back. 'I'm trying to find out what turned you from the warm and giving woman I was holding in my arms a few minutes ago into the biting little witch you are right now!'

Her eyes flashed green sarcasm at him. 'Have dinner with me tonight and we'll discuss it.' She threw one of his own classic fob-offs at him, giving him a very good clue as to what had upset her at the same time.

And Mac was not slow. 'Ah,' he said. 'You're angry because I have to fly out to the States.'

'I'm angry,' she corrected him, 'because I've let you divert me once again from the course I am determined to take! Which is,' she added, before he could say a single word, 'to get your endorsement of that letter of resignation so I can finally break completely free from you!'

'Why bother when you know you don't really want to?' he deflected infuriatingly, then sighed when it looked as if she was about ready to explode with frustration. 'You're right,' he conceded, 'and this is getting out of hand. So I'll do us both a favour.' Reaching behind him, he picked up her letter and brought it to where they could both see it. 'If I do—this...' Smoothly he ripped her letter in two, while all Roberta could do was stand there and watch helplessly as the pieces fell discarded to the floor. 'Now all you have to do,' he went on calmly, 'is wait a whole week before typing out another one. By then I will be back from the States and we can discuss this more thoroughly—over dinner, as you proposed—and I will guarantee you—unreservedly,' he promised, laying a mocking hand over his heart, 'my whole and complete attention for whatever time it takes.'

'Unless the phone rings,' she grunted.

'Roberta!' he snapped with waning patience. 'I'm really trying to make this work for us—can't you see that?' he appealed.

'Why?' she said.

'Why?' Mac stared at her, nonplussed for a moment, then made a weary sound of surrender. 'I'm going to give up on this,' he decided, straightening up to stride over to her. 'Just promise to wait a week—one week!' he insisted as his hands took a forceful grip on her slender shoulders. 'Before you do anything about trying to leave here—please?' he begged, at her stubborn look. 'I don't want to go to the states right now but I *have* to go. There's a problem there that only I can sort out! But when I get back, I promise you, we'll talk. Talk seriously about us and where we're going to go from here.'

'But I don't see what good it will do!' she cried. 'We'll only continue to go around and around in circles again, as we always end up doing!'

'No, we won't,' he determined, and something in his eyes forced her to accept that he meant it. 'Not this time. A week, bunny rabbit.' He bent his head and kissed her gently. 'Be generous towards me for this one last time, and wait the week.'

On a heavy sigh, she closed her eyes. His gentle kiss, the husky plea and the sweet sound of his special name coming so intimately from his lips were melting her like butter inside, so that she didn't even know she'd said, 'OK,' until she heard the word slide off her tongue.

And it was only once she was standing on the other side of his door, with her eyes closed tightly over defeated eyes, that she acknowledged to herself that she had let him do it again. He had talked her round yet again—seduced her round yet again!

CHAPTER NINE

THE next week was a busy one. Joel had started a new project, and she became bogged down in laborious investigative work. Mac didn't ring, but then she hadn't expected him to. What had to be said between them was too important to be touched upon via a telephone connection, so it was better to have no contact at all.

So she lost herself in work and, to her surprise, managed to keep Mac right out of her thoughts for most of the time. Until Friday afternoon, that was, when she walked unannounced into Joel's office, needing to see him about something, only to come to a dead stop when she saw that Lulu was sitting there with him.

'Oh,' she said, momentarily stumped for once, 'I'm sorry to intrude,' and went to go away again.

Only Lulu stopped her, her lovely face alight with malicious derision. 'If it isn't Daddy's lady-friend,' she drawled. 'Or should I say *ex*-lady-friend?'

'Lulu!' Joel's sharp reprimand by no means compared with the sudden burn that began in the pit of Roberta's stomach.

Yet she still managed to hang on to her self-control, her voice, when she spoke, belying the storm of prickly anger clambering right across the surface of her skin. And, other than sending Lulu a withering look, she fixed her attention exclusively on Joel.

'I'll come back later, Joel, when you're not busy.'

'No—Roberta, wait.' Joel came to his feet, his expression tight with anger as he stayed her with a gesturing hand. 'You deserve an apology from this ill-mannered young lady, and she is going to give it to you—aren't you, Lulu?' he prompted threateningly.

Lulu's beautiful lavender-blue eyes opened wide in utter contempt. 'No, I'm not,' she refused. 'And really, Uncle Joel,' she murmured deridingly, 'I don't know how you can keep her working here with you now that Daddy has seen fit to throw her out!'

'That's enough!' Joel rasped while Roberta turned to leave, counting very slowly to ten to stop herself from retaliating. 'How dare you speak to Roberta like that?' he demanded. 'How dare you?'

'She dares,' Roberta heard herself say grimly, 'because she has been allowed to believe she can dare.' Turning, she faced the room again, her gaze as hard as tightly packed ice. 'But I do think it's time that someone put you right on a few pertinent points, Miss Maclaine,' she continued coldly. 'The main one being that your father did not throw me out of his life and never has!'

'Liar,' Lulu jeered. 'I was there, remember? At the hospital when Mummy was ill? I heard him tell you to get out!'

'What you heard,' Roberta amended, 'was your father wanting to remove me from the shame his daughter made him feel for her!' And she knew as she said it—knew that that was exactly what Mac had been doing. He hadn't been telling her to get out because he believed Lulu's lies, but because he couldn't stand having her listen to them!

Lulu jumped to her feet, that wildness back in her eyes. 'He hates you!' she hissed out malevolently. 'He told me so!'

'Sit down,' Roberta commanded quietly. 'Sit down!' she repeated forcefully, putting a hand on the younger

girl's shoulder to push her down when she did not respond to the order.

'Roberta——' Joel murmured warningly.

'Stay out of this, Joel,' she clipped, not taking her
eyes off the younger woman. 'This is between Lulu and
me. I've put up with the insults from her vile tongue
long enough. But, more than that, I've finished with the
lies. Finished with them—do you hear, Lulu?' she demanded. 'And for once in your spoiled life you're going
to listen for a change, listen to me telling you a few choice
but bitter home-truths.'

'I don't have to sit here and listen to a single word
you have to say,' Lulu countered shakily, beginning to
look a little wary of this new, coldly furious Roberta she
had never seen before.

'You do,' Roberta assured her. 'Because I am going
to make sure you do. Your father has never so much as
tried to throw me out of his life,' she stated. 'But,' she
went on, 'I've walked out on your father because I could
not stand the vileness of his bigoted family for a minute
longer!'

'You're the liar!' Lulu said again. 'He threw you out!
He always throws them out, because I make sure he . . .'

Joel's horrified gasp brought that little truth to an
abrupt end. But it came too late to save Lulu and she
knew it, which was why her face went red, her eyes
flashing bright blue with guilt.

'Which makes you—what, exactly?' Roberta asked,
compounding on the error with quiet contempt in her
voice. 'Mean, Lulu. It makes you a mean, spoiled, utterly selfish child.'

'I hate you!' Lulu retaliated, pushing her angry face
up close to Roberta's. 'All my family hates you! You
wanted to split my parents up and——'

'Split them up?' Joel choked in disbelief. 'Are you crazy, Lulu? They've been apart for over eight years!'

'What I can't understand,' Roberta went on, as if the other two had not spoken, 'is how anyone who has had such an amount of tender, loving care lavished on them can end up as bitter and twisted as you. But, having become what you are, Lucinda——' she gave her her full name simply because she knew Lulu hated it, and in the quiet part of her burning brain recognised that that was her own form of maliciousness coming out '—I think it's high time you took a good look at the finished product. You are, without doubt,' she told her, 'the most selfish-minded person it has ever been my misfortune to meet. You are so self-motivated that you don't even care how miserable you make those around you feel, so long as they make sure that you, above all, feel loved!'

'That's not true!' Lulu choked. 'I'm not——'

'Selfish?' Roberta prompted. 'In the way you constantly make your father prove his love for you by forcing him to pretend he has no private life beyond the tight family group? Mean—in the way you won't let him find happiness his own way, without making him feel cruel and guilty? Or malicious—in the way you've treated me and the others before me that you're so proud of getting rid of?'

'Roberta...' Joel put in pleadingly when he saw his niece's face turn greyer with each thrust.

'And finally, Lulu,' she said harshly, 'jealous—of anything or anyone who dares threaten what you see as your power over him. And all for what?' she asked as she straightened away, her eyes pale with contempt. 'To punish a man who, because he loves you from the bottom of his heart, put up with a marriage that was sour even

before it began for ten wretched years, before he found
he couldn't stand the misery of it any more and got out.
But that doesn't interest you, does it?' she scoffed. 'Because to take into consideration your father's feelings
would mean that you would have to put your own aside,
and you're just too mean to try.'

'Y-you're only saying all this to me because you're
peeved that he'll never marry you,' Lulu said shakily,
coming unsteadily to her feet.

'Marriage?' Roberta laughed, a short, huffing laugh
that showed her utter derision of the word. 'I would truly
have to be the empty-headed bimbo you like to believe
I am to want to marry into a family like yours. No, Lulu.'
She shook her head. 'I don't want marriage from your
father. I don't want anything from him—not any more,'
she added bleakly. 'You see, I want the man I marry to
be strong. I want him to love me above all others. And
your father can never be either of those things while he's
still so irremovably tied to your leading-reins.'

'Bitch!' Lulu spat out viciously.

But all Roberta did was smile. 'Well, at least that's
one up on being a bimbo, isn't it?' she drawled, and
calmly walked out of the room.

'Wow!' Mitzy drawled as Roberta walked past her,
having obviously listened in on the whole thing.

'Shut up!' she clipped, and shut herself in her own
office, walked around her desk and sat down determinedly to hand-write her second letter of resignation
in a week.

Only this one she meant to make Mac accept, she
thought grimly.

'Joel took Lulu home,' Mitzy informed her, sidling
warily into the office several minutes later. 'He said to

tell you that he wasn't coming back until Mac had been and gone, the coward.'

Mac? Roberta frowned. Did that mean Mac was back in London?

'Arrived this lunchtime,' Mitzy said, as if she could read Roberta's thoughts. 'I had lunch with his secretary,' she explained her source of information. 'She said he was going straight home to sleep off the jet-lag.'

Roberta felt a swift sting of alarm shoot down her spine. She hadn't given a thought to what Mac's reaction was going to be when he found out she had attacked his daughter.

But she did now, so she was more or less ready for him when he came through the door just an hour later.

'Who the hell do you think you are,' he grated, 'speaking to my daughter like that?'

She looked up at him, was surprised to see that he looked less than neat in creased suit trousers, no jacket or tie, and his white shirt wrenched open at the throat by what looked like very impatient fingers. He looked pale and tired too, the classic symptoms of jet-lag.

'Well?' he bit out, when she didn't instantly jump to her own defence.

'Are you referring to the few home-truths I felt it was time she listened to?' she asked coolly, and watched with detached interest as the lid flew right off his temper.

'You crazy, vindictive bitch!' he rasped. 'This was your way of paying her back for lying about you to me, wasn't it?'

'No,' she denied the accusation, sounding as calm as still waters while he was stirring up a storm. 'It was my way of paying her back for daring to insult me once too often,' she amended.

'That's all?' he bit out, coming to lean threateningly on her desk. 'You spit a load of abuse at her and reduce her to a shivering heap of tears because she insulted you? She's only a child, dammit! A poor, mixed-up child!'

'Child?' Roberta made a sound of disgust. 'Oh, do open your eyes, Mac! She is an eighteen-year-old teenager who has an unhealthy obsession about her father!'

'Why, you——!' His hand snaked out, fingers curling tightly around the back of her neck to lift her to her feet. Thunder roared in the air around him, his eyes silver-bright, burning into hers. 'How dare you suggest anything so vile?'

'Take your hand off me before I shout for Mitzy to call security,' she warned.

For an answer the fingers tightened their hold. 'You mean as I should do for the way you attacked the chairman's daughter?'

'Oh, pulling rank again, are we?' she scoffed at that remark. 'Well, you just try it, Mac,' she challenged, holding back the urge to wince at his hurtful grip. 'And even though you're their revered employer they would laugh in your face once they'd heard the full story. Which I would be only too happy to tell them,' she warned, then asked softly, 'Are you man enough to listen to it, Mac? Or has Lulu got you too tied up in knots with her own twisted version?'

His angry eyes flashed, and Roberta held her breath, waiting tensely to see which way he would jump. He wanted to murder her; she could see it boiling in his eyes. But underneath—deep down beneath—Mac had to know that she would not have done anything to Lulu without extreme provocation.

He let go, turning his back on her as Roberta dropped weakly back into her chair. She was trembling so badly

that even her heart felt as if it was shaking, and she
lifted a hand up to rub her neck, her own tension as
much as his grip making it ache.

'Talk,' he commanded gruffly, and went to stand over
by the window. Roberta followed him with her eyes,
almost letting herself feel sorry for him, he looked so
utterly fed up. But she stiffened her spine. She was sick
and tired of being the kicking-board both for him and
his possessive family. And, whether or not he believed
her after this, at least she would have got a whole lot of
simmering resentment off her chest.

'All right,' she said, sitting back in her chair, 'where
would you like me to begin? With the first time I ever
met Lulu as your lover and she warned me then that I
wouldn't last a month if she had anything to do with it?
Or,' she continued as he swung around to frown at her,
'shall we just jump forward to her recent birthday party,
when she took great pleasure in stalking me around the
room, explaining to anyone who would listen—within
my hearing, of course—just who I was. "Daddy's current
bimbo".' Her mouth thinned with distaste on the words.
'Or,' she went on, ignoring his narrowing stare, 'shall
we remove to the little scene at the hospital, when she
tried—very hard—to convince me that you still slept with
Delia when you got the chance?'

Mac went pale and turned away from her again. The
fact that he wasn't jumping all over her for being a liar
eased some of the tension out of her as she continued
quietly, 'Don't think I'm putting the blame entirely on
to Lulu. She had a lot of encouragement, after all, from
both you and Delia. You both put on such a convincing
show, you see.' She sighed. 'It's no wonder Lulu waits
with bated breath for the day when you suddenly see
sense and remarry her mother.' In profile, she saw his

bitter grimace, and knew he was accepting what she was saying. 'Delia, on the other hand, I'm not so sure about,' she went on. 'I think she plays the game in a similar way to you. But I could be wrong, and maybe she too is simply waiting in the wings for you to turn back to her. I don't know.'

Mac sighed, running his hand around the back of his neck before he dropped it again and came over to throw himself into the chair across the desk from her.

'You'd better tell me the rest,' he invited wearily. 'What happened in Joel's office today?'

Anger darkened Roberta's eyes for a moment, then cleared as she controlled it. 'I walked into Joel's office to find Lulu already there. My first instinct was to get back out again as quickly as my legs would take me,' she wryly confessed, 'but Lulu attacked first, and...' With a helpless shrug she told him all of it, the lot, barely missing anything out. 'And if you don't believe me,' she concluded, 'then just ask Joel—or even Mitzy, come to that, because I think she overheard the whole ugly thing!'

Restlessly she got up, going to take up Mac's angry pose by the window. 'In trying to keep your daughter's love you've created a monster,' she told him flatly. 'And if you don't do something about it very soon, Mac, then I think it may just be too late—for poor Lulu, at any rate.' Turning her head, she looked grimly at him. 'She isn't happy, you know,' she said gently. 'She can never be happy while she continues to believe that her whole happiness hinges on getting her parents back together.'

'We won't do that. Never,' he grunted, with a small shudder that seemed to say it all.

'Then don't you think it's time one or both of you told her that?' Roberta suggested. 'I know I don't like your daughter very much,' she admitted, with her usual unfailing honesty, 'but having watched what goes on from the outside, so to speak, I do have it in me to understand why she continues to hope.'

He sighed, stretching out in the upright chair and throwing back his head with his eyes closed. He looked wearied to death.

Roberta's eyes flooded with tears, because she was painfully aware that she was responsible for making him like that. But she turned back to the window, refusing to let herself respond even though the urge to go over and soothe him throbbed achingly inside her. She had regretted her part in the scene with Lulu almost before she had walked out of Joel's office, but, having had the confrontation, she knew she would be being a fool to herself if she retracted any of it just to ease Mac's feelings.

'I think it's time I explained to you something about Lulu,' he murmured suddenly, drawing her attention back to him. 'About three years ago she got in with a bad crowd. Went so wild for a time that Delia couldn't control her. She even began stealing from the house—oh, not big things,' he allowed, at Roberta's stifled gasp, 'but small things, things that wouldn't be missed straight away but would fetch her a reasonable price on the street.' He paused, his mouth folding into a grim, tight line. 'She was selling them for drugs—nothing heavy,' he added. 'Luckily, I found out what she was up to before she'd progressed on to anything seriously damaging. She's clear now—is even embarrassed if it ever comes up. But...' There was another pause, followed by another harsh sigh while Roberta stood there, feeling helpless as to what to say. 'During the therapy she agreed to attend it came out that she was still feeling rejected by me for leaving her and Delia. So I suppose that, since then, Delia and I have got used to putting up a united front whenever she's around and, like you said, so successfully that Lulu has misread its meaning.' He opened his eyes to pin her with a sombre look. 'But I hadn't realised how much until I overheard all those things she was saying to you that morning at the hospital.'

'You heard her?' Roberta gasped.

'Not just heard her, but tackled her about it afterwards,' he admitted. 'Then, to be honest, I just lost patience with her. I thought to myself——' grimly he lurched forward '—what the hell am I doing, putting my life on hold for her when she can lie so bloody glibly about me like that?' He gave his dark head a small shake. 'She apologised afterwards,' he went on. 'Explained why she'd said some of the rotten things she'd said to you. Half of it was her own conscience, refusing to accept responsibility for any part of her mother's illness. Delia, you see, had told Lulu that she felt sick before the party. But Lulu had begged her not to tell anyone so that her weekend wouldn't be spoiled by everyone worrying about Delia!' His anger and disgust showed in the rasping tone of his voice. 'So discovering just how ill Delia was and how close to death Delia came by not doing something about herself sooner came as a real leveller to her—so naturally,' he added sarcastically, 'she took it out on the nearest person to hand, which happened to be you—or maybe it was only because it was you.' He sighed. 'Whatever. It was you who got it in the neck, and me who had to stand there listening to you get it!'

'So you sent me away,' she murmured softly.

'Had to,' he gritted. 'However angry I was with Lulu, her mother was seriously ill, and I had to wait for the outcome there before I could even begin to tackle her outburst to you. What really surprises me,' he said frowningly, 'is that, after all of that, she dared to start on you again today.'

'She hates me,' Roberta murmured heavily. 'She's a typically selfish eighteen-year-old, who would hate and resent anyone trying to spoil what she sees as her ultimate plan in life. Which is to get you and Delia back together again.'

Mac leaned forward to rest his elbows on his spread knees, sighing in weary acceptance of that. 'Can you get Mitzy to make me some coffee?' he then asked suddenly. 'Only, I'd just walked in the door from New York when Lulu rang me to pour all your insults over me, and to be frank——' he grimaced. 'I'm bloody spent.'

'Of course,' she said, glad of something to do other than listen and think and hurt for all of them.

She stepped over to her desk and buzzed Mitzy for coffee then, after hovering for a few moments, fighting a battle with herself, rounded the desk to go down on her haunches beside him, her weak heart winning out over stern resolve to keep herself aloof from him.

But he looked so endearingly vulnerable sitting there, slumped over like that, and her hand went tentatively to his cheek, unsure whether she would be rejected or not. But, far from rejecting her, he took the hand into his own, kissed her fingers gently, then kept it captured as he lowered it down to her lap.

'I have a lot to apologise to you for, don't I?' he murmured gruffly.

Roberta smiled, watching the way he played absently with her fingers. 'Not really,' she denied. 'I probably deserved most of what I got, simply because I allowed it to go on.'

'Until Lulu's party,' he said. 'When you suddenly found you'd had enough.'

More than enough, she thought, remembering painfully how those words had hit her full in the face that night.

He moved so unexpectedly that Roberta started in puzzled surprise as he climbed to his feet to begin pacing the room, suddenly the dark, restless man she was more used to seeing. He was thinking, she realised, coming more slowly to her own feet. He'd recovered from the shock and was now doing what he did best: looking for the best solution to solve the problem.

Mitzy came in with a tray of coffee, eyeing him warily as she put it down on Roberta's desk then disappeared as quickly as she could. Roberta didn't have a chance to pour the coffee before Mac was there and doing it himself. He gulped down two cupfuls, black, strong and sweet, before pacing away again. She watched him, this powerhouse method of thinking exciting her even though she knew she shouldn't let it.

But this was Mac. Mac the man she'd fallen in love with. Mac the man who could turn all of this restless energy into pure, undiluted passion. And her mouth went dry at the idea of it, her body stirring into tight, tingling shocks of awareness.

Wicked, she accused herself breathlessly. Wicked— wicked! Mac is dealing with a big problem in his life and you're standing here wanting to devour him.

He turned suddenly, catching her hungry look, but thankfully too preoccupied to recognise it for the wicked thing it was. Instead he strode over to the desk and snatched up the phone, sharp fingers punching in a well-remembered set of numbers. 'Delia?' he said almost instantly.

Something cracked inside Roberta. He was calling his ex-wife. Mac had come to a big decision about something, and she had a horrible feeling that she knew what that decision was.

'Is Lulu still there?' He sounded so brisk and alive that Roberta wanted to weep. 'What?' he drawled. 'Already?' His mouth took on a rueful twist. 'It didn't take her long to recover, did it?'

Whatever Delia said by way of reply made his expression harden. 'It's sorted, Delia. More than sorted,' he said grimly, glancing at Roberta in a way that made her sure they were discussing her. So in response her chin went up, green eyes spiralling into cool challenge. Yet, oddly, he smiled at her, before returning his attention to the telephone. 'How are you feeling, darling?' he enquired of Delia, reminding Roberta that Delia must still be recovering from her operation. 'Only, I think you should know that we have a small crisis brewing and we urgently need to talk about it.' Delia said something that made his face darken. 'No,' he muttered. 'Not just Lulu, but you and me, too. May I come round in, say——' he glanced at his watch '—half an hour?'

She must have agreed because Mac nodded and put down the receiver, then, with a decidedly threatening look about him, turned his attention on Roberta. 'Right,' he said. 'Where's Joel?'

She was instantly on her guard. 'Out,' she answered. 'Hiding away from you, I think.'

'Is he, now?' he murmured. 'That'll make a change. Usually he enjoys taking me on! Like the time in Jenny's flat when he provoked me into punching him one.'

'That was a disgraceful thing to do!' she flared. 'Hitting your own brother just because he made a very poor joke!'

'That's my bunny rabbit,' he drawled. 'Defend the in-defensible. He envies me you, no matter what you prefer to believe.'

She stiffened instantly in affront. 'I don't see how you——'

She got no further because his mouth came hungrily down on her own. 'Mmm,' he murmured as he drew away. 'I needed that!'

Roberta just stared at him in breathless bewilderment. He was so bright and alive now that she could hardly believe that this was the same man who had been slumped in a chair in defeat only minutes ago!

'Now, where's your coat?' he asked, looking impatiently round the room. 'Get your coat. You're coming with me.'

'I most certainly am not!' Roberta protested, staring at him as if he'd gone stark, staring mad. 'Just in case it's escaped your memory, I work here!' she reminded him hotly. 'I can't just walk out at a moment's notice, even if I wanted to—which I don't!'

'I'm the boss, remember? So get your coat!' Grabbing determinedly at her hand, he took it upon himself to hook her coat off the hanger behind her door, then threw it over his shoulder. 'We have things to do, you and I,' he stated. 'And, now I've decided to do them, I want them doing right away.'

'Things like what?' she demanded in exasperation. 'Mac!' she appealed, when he began dragging her protestingly through the door. 'I don't want to go with you to Delia's! And I don't see why you would want me along!'

'Don't you?' He kept on pulling. 'You started all of this, Roberta,' he reminded her grimly. 'So I don't see why the hell you shouldn't help me to finish it!'

'Finish what?' she sighed out bewilderedly. 'Can't you just stand still long enough to tell me what the hell it is you're intending to do?'

He shook his head. 'You'll find out soon enough,' he promised ominously. At Mitzy's desk, though, he paused. 'If you know which hole it is that my brother is hiding in, then get him out of it and tell him that I've kidnapped his PA,' he instructed a Mitzy wide-eyed with curiosity. 'Tell him that if he wants to see Miss Chandler again, then he'd better come and find her. At Delia's.' He glanced at his watch. 'Just as soon as he can get himself there.'

'This is crazy,' Roberta complained as he drove them towards the St John's Wood district of London, after having dragged her out of the building, shoved her into his car, then belted her in before slamming the door and climbing in himself. 'You've gone crazy if you think you can just bully me like this!'

He just ignored her, driving the new-model Lotus with the cool precision of a lion-tamer controlling a wild animal. Delia's home was the one Mac had once shared with her. A big old thing, set behind a high fence in its own secluded grounds. The heavy wrought-iron gates opened electronically and it niggled Roberta to know that Mac still had right of access, when, at the touch of a button on his dashboard, the gates slid open to let them drive through.

He stopped at the bottom of the stone front steps which led beneath a wide porchway, killed the engine, then climbed out, came around to open Roberta's door for her when she made no effort herself, and firmly hauled her out.

'I have no wish to go in there!' she informed him hotly.

'No matter,' he said, his hand a manacle about hers again as he pulled her towards the steps. 'You're coming.'

Inside was quite surprisingly conservative, Delia's exotic tastes in personal dress obviously not overlapping into her taste in home décor.

A tall, grey-haired man with a sober face came to meet them as they entered. 'Where's your mistress, Jock?' Mac asked him.

'In the small sitting-room, sir,' the man replied. 'Resting,' he added pointedly.

Mac just grunted at the other man's acid manner and walked off down the hall, dragging Roberta behind him.

Delia was reclining on a beautiful damask-covered sofa, her silky red hair flowing like lava over the softly padded arm. She looked wonderful in that particular shade of violet satin she had strategically draped around her—exotic, seductive—and Roberta suddenly realised why the house was so elegantly bland. It acted as the perfect foil to Delia's hectic beauty.

'How's the wound?' Mac asked by way of a greeting.

'Healing,' Delia informed him, without bothering to open her delicately bruised eyes. 'But killing me. What's all this urgency about, Mac?' she demanded wearily. 'I suppose that sly bitch has been making trouble for poor Lulu?'

'Ask her yourself, since the bitch in question is standing right next to me,' Mac drawled, watching cynically as Delia's eyes flicked wide open while Roberta stiffened jerkily at his side. 'And as for poor Lulu,' he continued, while both women glared at each other, 'we've let a serious problem develop between us here, Delia, and it's high time we did something about it.'

'Problem? What kind of problem?' Wincing at the effort, Delia levered herself into a sitting position.

For an answer, Mac stunned both women. 'Will you marry me, Delia?' he asked.

'You must be joking!' Delia scoffed, without even having to think about it. 'I wouldn't do that to myself again even if you were the last man on earth!'

'Good,' Mac said. 'Which gets that bit out of the way, since the last thing on earth I want to do is tie myself to a witch like you again. So,' he went on, tugging at Roberta's hand until he had her hard up against his side, 'I will have your full support when I announce that Roberta and I are getting married, won't I?'

CHAPTER TEN

SILENCE. Mac's cool announcement met with total, utter silence from both stunned women while they struggled to absorb just exactly what he'd said.

It was Delia who recovered first, while Roberta ran his arrogant remark over and over in her mind, trying to work out how she had misheard what she thought he'd said. But, staring at Mac with something close to horror, Delia whispered threadily, 'Oh, hell, Mac. This will cause something really nasty to hit the fan!'

'No!' Roberta burst out, coming alive at last to wrench herself free from Mac's grasp. 'Who the hell do you think you are, dragging me here like this and making arrogant assumptions like that?' she cried, her face as pale as her beautiful hair. 'I won't marry you!' she declared. 'I don't want to marry you—I don't even like you, or your horrible family!'

'Well, that's telling you, sweet-face,' Delia mocked Mac, looking as if she was suddenly enjoying herself.

'And you can go to hell, too,' Roberta told her crossly, wrapping her arms tightly around herself. It was either that or hit one of them. And she'd done enough lashing out today, even if it was only with her tongue. More than enough, she then extended, grimly aware that, if she'd just held on to her self-control and walked out on Lulu before, she wouldn't be in this situation now!

'I've been there already, darling, believe me,' Delia drawled. 'In actual fact, Mac and I visited the place together.'

'And stayed there ten damn years too long,' he agreed, wry amusement sounding in his voice.

These two were crazy! Roberta decided, flicking her impatient gaze from one warmly laughing face to the other. They talked to each other like enemies, yet the affection—real, genuine affection for each other—glowed through each clever, taunting word!

Then jealousy ripped through her like the very flames of hell, because they were too busy teasing each other even to remember she was there! I want him to look at me like that! she thought angrily. I want him to laugh with me! Care for me! I want him to ask me to marry him because he desperately wants me to and not because of some devious plan he's cooked up to put his stupid daughter in her place!

'I'm leaving,' she announced, turning towards the door.

'Like hell you are,' Mac growled, reaching out to bring her to a jerking halt. 'You started this and my God you're going to stay and help finish it!'

'Finish what?' a carefully monitored voice enquired from the open doorway.

Joel! Roberta recognised with relief. Joel would get her out of this! 'Tell him, Joel!' she pleaded, pulling at her captured wrist. 'Tell this big bully to get his hands off me!'

'I would let go of her if I were you, Mac,' Joel suggested quietly. And it was in his eyes that he meant it. 'Don't you think you're a bit big to go around threatening women?'

'I'm not threatening her, dammit!' Mac snapped impatiently. 'I'm trying to marry her!'

'Marry?' Joel's expression could not have taken on a bigger change if it had tried. 'Oh, that's all right, then,'

he said, and proceeded to ignore Roberta as he came
further into the room. 'I was beginning to think you
hadn't got the guts! But now I see you have—put it there,
big brother!' He held out a hand to Mac. 'I hope you've
ordered me round here to ask me to be best man?'

'Stop it!' Roberta choked, very close to a flood of
angry tears. 'Will you all please just stop it?'

Big arms came warmly round her, hugging her close
to a big, warm, infinitely familiar body. 'Don't cry,
bunny rabbit,' a deep voice soothed. 'Everything will
turn out all right. You'll see.'

'But I can't marry you, Mac—can't you see?' Lifting
tear-washed eyes to his, she pleaded for him to stop this
madness. 'Your daughter doesn't like me! And since you
both still seem to live in each other's pockets,' she added,
flashing a jealous green glance at Delia, 'then the fact
that your ex-wife doesn't like me seems to put the lid on
such a stupid idea!'

'But I like you,' Mac murmured, eyes full of tender
laughter as he gently combed his fingers through her silky
hair. 'I like you very, very much...' he told her, and
kissed her—not slowly, not gently, but strongly, with a
hungry passion that had her senses spinning and her body
arching helplessly to his.

She didn't even care that Delia was looking on, that
Joel was watching and probably smirking. She didn't
care that Mac was taking unfair advantage and she
should be fighting like mad to get free, because in the
end—on the very bottom line of it—she knew that this
was where she wanted to be, where she needed to be.

'I still can't marry you,' she whispered against his lips,
when he eventually eased the pressure. 'They'd make my
life a misery if I did.'

'You mean Lulu,' he specified.

She nodded, her unhappy eyes lost in the dark beauty of his. 'She's your daughter and you love her, and I won't let you hurt her through me.' The tears flooded her eyes again. 'She'd never forgive me if I did!' she choked.

'Yes, I would.'

Four heads spun round to see Lulu standing in the open doorway, looking awkward and defensive with her fingers stuck into the tight front pockets of her jeans. Instinct made Roberta want to take a defensive step away from Mac, but he tightened his hold, keeping her close.

Ruthless bastard, she told him silently. Now you've decided to deal with Lulu, you're going to pull no punches, are you?

Lulu glanced at her father's suddenly closed face, then at Roberta's very wary one, and grimaced, her gaze then clashing with her uncle Joel's for a long moment before her dark lashes swept down over her beautiful eyes. And it hit Roberta then that Joel must have done some hard talking to Lulu to make her look at him like that.

'I think I've been making rather a nuisance of myself,' she said, sidling further into the room, then added with a small shrug, 'I'm—sorry.'

'Oh, Lulu, darling,' Delia murmured with a quiver in her voice.

Lulu glanced at her and smiled, albeit ruefully. 'It's your own fault, you know—both your faults,' she added, including her father in the remark. 'You always manage to look so—right together!' Another shrug, then her slender shoulders sagged. 'Anyone could be forgiven for thinking you were nothing but a silly pair of children who just had too much pride to kiss and make up!'

If Delia gasped at being spoken to like that by her daughter, Joel huffed out a sardonic laugh. 'Good for you, pug-face,' he encouraged. 'You tell them what you think of them; it's about time somebody did!'

'Somebody already did, Uncle Joel,' Lulu reminded him. 'Told me, anyway.' And she turned to look directly at Roberta. 'Do you love my father?' she demanded outright.

The room seemed to sway, and Roberta had to close her eyes in an attempt to stop it. Why did she have to ask me that question? she thought hectically. Why couldn't she ask it of her arrogant father instead? His answer would be far more interesting, since everyone but Lulu, it seemed, knew her feelings! His were still a damned closed book!

The arms enfolding her tightened. 'Well, come on, bunny rabbit,' Mac whispered gently. 'Answer the girl and let's just see if that unfailing honesty of yours stands up in a real test!'

'I hate you,' she whispered, opening her eyes directly on to his warmly teasing gaze. 'I hate all your rotten family!'

'Mmm. I know,' he agreed, and kissed the tip of her small, straight nose. 'But...?' he then prompted.

Pain shot across her features, pain and despair and a wretched weak surrender. 'But I can't help loving you too,' she shakily confessed.

'Then you both have my blessing when you marry,' Lulu murmured in a thickened voice that said it hurt her to say it.

'Oh, I'm not going to marry him!' Roberta stunned everyone by declaring, and looked stubbornly into Mac's suddenly narrowed eyes. 'I'm not marrying you, Mac,' she repeated, and gently but firmly withdrew herself from his arms, wanting—needing to get away before she fell apart inside.

'But why?' Lulu cried, glancing at her father's face and going pale at whatever she saw written there. She moved jerkily to stand in front of Roberta. 'You said you wanted him strong!' she reminded her. 'Well, hasn't he proved he can be strong by asking you to marry him even though he knows it would hurt me?'

Roberta's heavy sigh drowned out the shorter, shocked one Mac gave. 'It's nothing to do with strength,' she denied wearily.

'Then it's me.' Lulu reached out to grab her arm when Roberta went to turn away. 'You don't want me as a stepdaughter. I can understand that!' she cried painfully. 'After all, who would? I'm such a terrible bitch! But——!'

'Stop it, Lulu,' Mac inserted grimly, but his daughter just turned wide, urgent eyes on him.

'No!' she refused. 'I won't stop it! This is all my fault and I won't stop it until I make it all right with you two again! Roberta,' she pleaded urgently, unconsciously using her name for the first time ever, 'if I promise not to interfere one tiny little bit, will you marry him? I'll stay right out of your lives if you prefer!' Sincere though she was being, her lovely eyes filled with tears at the prospect and, despite all the antagonism they'd shared during the last twelve months, Roberta couldn't let the other girl hurt herself like this.

She took hold of her shoulders and, even though they were already trembling, gave them a gentle shake. 'My decision has nothing to do with you, Lulu!' she assured her. 'It has to do with love—pure and simple—nothing else! Your father doesn't love me, darling,' she explained softly. 'Didn't you know that?'

'Are you crazy or something?' Mac burst in explosively. 'When the hell have I ever said I didn't love you?'

'When have you ever said you did?' Roberta corrected him grimly.

'You mean, he's never even told you?' Lulu gasped. 'You mean, the selfish rat has just taken and taken without bothering to——'

'Lulu!'

This time Mac's harsh reprimand brought her tongue to a skidding halt, but her eyes, when she lanced them on him, condemned, and Mac's face darkened with colour.

'I'm getting out of here,' Roberta said, taking her chance while father and daughter spat knives at each other.

'Good,' Mac said. 'I'm coming with you.'

'But she doesn't want you to!' Lulu told him fiercely.

'Darling.' Mac paused in front of his daughter and bent to kiss her angry cheek. 'I love you more than life itself, so don't be offended when I tell you that you haven't got the faintest idea what Roberta wants. But I do,' he said huskily, swinging an arm around Roberta's stiff shoulders. 'She wants convincing. She wants coaxing. She wants me to grovel and beg, and a whole lot of other things that are just too shocking for your delicate ears. So we will both wish you all good-day,' he concluded lightly, using brute strength to make Roberta move towards the door with him, 'and we'll see you all again one night next week, at my apartment, with a full complement of Maclaines and——' He paused to look enquiringly at Roberta. 'Are your parents still in the country?'

'Yes,' she frowned. 'But——'

'Your aunt Sadie? The two miserable uncles?' he cut in.

'Yes!' she sighed. 'But——'

He looked away from her. 'Then it will be a full complement of Maclaines *and* Chandlers present to help celebrate our coming nuptials!'

With that, he marched her out of the room. 'Will you get your damned hand off me?' she demanded, tugging frustratingly while he pulled.

'When you're safely in the car,' he answered, dragging her outside and down the steps. 'Get in,' he ordered, once he'd opened the car door.

She shook her head stubbornly, digging her heels in. 'I am not marrying you, Mac!' she repeated coolly. 'You can tug and bully me around as much as you like but you won't make me change my mind.'

'Get in the car,' was all he said.

'I...'

'Get in the car,' he repeated, then, in a quite unexpected explosion, '*Get in the damned car, woman*! *Get in the car*!' His accompanying fist coming down hard on the roof of his precious Lotus made her jump, her green eyes widening in startled surprise. Oh, he could shout with the best of them, she allowed; he could even bang about a bit in rage, but she had never actually seen him lose his temper quite so spectacularly before.

'What's the matter with you?' she gasped, stunned out of her own anger.

The darkening flash of his eyes was the only warning she got before she found herself crushed in his arms and being kissed with a vengeance. By the time he released her, she was feeling so dizzy that she could barely support herself.

'Not strong enough for you, am I not?' he taunted grimly into the fluffy softness of her hair.

So that was it! she realised. It had hit a raw nerve when Lulu had repeated that choice little remark! 'I wasn't referring to your physical strength!' she informed him scornfully.

'My sexual strength, then?' he suggested.

'That,' she snapped, 'has never been in question—has it?' And even as she said it she felt that special tightening, deep in her stomach, that always betrayed her whenever she thought of Mac in any sexual way.

'The strength of my love, then,' he said, oh, so gently that it brought her eyes up to clash with the sudden, stomach-churningly seriousness of his. 'And I do love you, Roberta,' he added with soft sincerity. 'It's just that it took me a long time to realise it, that's all.'

'And that's supposed to make it OK?' she demanded, despite the declaration not in a forgiving mood at all. 'Because you realised, eventually, that you could well love me I am now supposed to fall gratefully into your arms and tell you that it doesn't matter that you've treated me terribly for the last twelve months? How conceited can you get?' she demanded in disgust.

'Not much more, I agree,' he said ruefully. 'But, you see, I never really had to bother thinking about it until you were no longer there for me to just——' he shrugged '—drown myself in.'

'Neither is that an acceptable excuse,' she scorned.

'No.' Heavily he shook his head, then turned to lean back against the car, the hand scraping wearily through his hair making her ache because it reminded her of how tired he had been feeling in her office earlier. 'But it's the truth,' he stated flatly. 'And you deserve nothing less than the truth from me. As for Lulu,' he added, then paused to let a long sigh rasp from him, his gaze flickering over the lovely Georgian house standing so graciously behind her, 'I love her,' he said simply. 'Hurting her hurt me too, so I did it as little as I possibly could. But——' a shrug of his wide shoulders brought his gaze back to settle on her '—I found it hurt me more to be without you,' he confessed, levelling meltingly serious eyes on her. 'I'm a selfish bastard, you know that,' he went on gravely, 'and I saw you as mine. My property. My woman!' he stated drily. 'But I didn't realise how much I was yours until you were no longer there to hold on to me! And I wanted you to hold on—tight!' His fingers tightened on her waist. 'So tight that I could never get away! And suddenly I didn't give a damn about my family!' he confessed. 'I didn't give a damn about anything but getting you back.'

'But on getting me back,' Roberta inserted, 'it didn't take long for family to claim precedence again, did it?'

'Are we talking about Zurich?' he sighed.

'Yes, we're talking about Zurich!' she snapped. 'You used me that night, Mac! No matter how you want to dress the whole thing up with words. You used me and were prepared to walk right out on me again when family duty called, no matter how that hurt me! If I hadn't pushed you to take me with you, you would not have suggested it yourself!'

'I know,' he sighed, looking weary again. 'But allowing you to come with me didn't do either of us much good in the end, did it?' He grimaced. 'Because Lulu staged a scene and you took off on your heels.'

'You told me to leave,' she reminded him.

'I meant the hospital, not the damned country!' he rasped. 'Have you any idea what it felt like to me that night, to come looking for you at Jenny's only to find you not there?'

'Niggled, did it?' she taunted. 'Not having me waiting at your beck and call?'

'Niggled? It worried me!' he bit out. 'I knew you'd left the hospital upset! I knew you'd most probably misinterpreted what I'd said. It was ages before I thought of ringing your parents' house, then, when I did, I got your father,' he said tightly, 'coolly telling me that he hadn't seen you in months.'

Roberta stared at him, aghast. 'My father?' she gasped. 'You spoke to my father and he said that? When?' she demanded breathlessly.

He shrugged. 'Early evening that same day,' he said.

'But he told me the call wasn't for me,' she murmured.

'So you didn't even know I'd rung?' Mac asked in surprise.

'No,' she said softly, her green eyes warming because, in his own way, her father had been protecting her from anything potentially hurtful, just as Mac tried to protect Lulu.

'That's why it came as such a surprise when you told me you'd been on holiday with them,' Mac explained, then asked curiously, 'What brought the holiday about?'

Roberta flushed, remembering, and looking away. 'Not telling,' she refused.

Mac began to grin, seeing the flush for exactly what it was. 'You were feeling wretched and told them all about me, didn't you?' he teased, lifting a finger to caress her jutting chin. 'I bet you told them what a bastard I am then admitted that you love me anyway, which is why they suddenly acquired protective instincts and told me lies. Am I right?' he prompted. 'Did you describe the big, bad wolf and Daddy got out his shotgun to kill him for you?'

'I am allowed a little tender, loving care myself, you know!' she flashed, goaded into doing so. 'Sweet Lulu doesn't have the monopoly on it!'

'From people who ignored you for the best part of your life?' he mocked. 'Come on, Roberta, you must have been shocked out of your mind when they responded like normal parents should do!'

'What's normal?' she countered. 'Do you class you and Delia as normal parents? Because I certainly don't, and I don't suppose Lulu does either!'

'True,' he conceded. 'I've never withheld love from her, though,' he pointed out. 'When I met you, bunny rabbit,' he added gently, 'you were totally and utterly starved of love.'

Tears spread across her eyes, because she knew he was right. 'That didn't mean you had to take advantage of it,' she choked.

'No,' he sighed, drawing her close. 'You're right. And that was the most painful truth that hit me full in the face that night in Zurich, when you begged me to take you with me,' he said. 'The truth that, unwittingly, or greedily, maybe,' he acknowledged heavily, 'I was starving you even more, the way I was using you.' His eyes darkened on her pained face. 'I can't turn back the clock, Roberta,' he murmured gruffly, 'but I can control the future from now on. If I promise to make you the axis that my whole world turns upon, can you forgive me enough to give me a second chance?'

A second chance? She almost laughed out loud at the ridiculousness of the plea. She would give him second chances, third and fourth, she was that much in love with him.

His hand lifted to her hair, gently stroking back a stray curl from one of her satin-smooth cheeks. 'I could kiss you into submission, you know,' he drawled. 'In two minutes flat I could have you so bent to my will that you'd let me take you right here in broad daylight on the concrete path!'

Her green eyes flashed. 'Touch you in a couple of strategic places and you're not so controlled yourself!' she retaliated. 'Even with the threat of your daughter, your ex-wife and your brother walking out here to catch you out!'

He grinned, not in the least bit ashamed of admitting his own weakness to her touch. 'Or we could go home,' he suggested warmly, 'go inside, lock the door, unplug the phone and see just who loses control first in the privacy of the bedroom, on a comfortable bed, with as many hours as we need to decide who is the winner without the smallest chance of interruption from anyone?'

'I'm still not going to marry you!' she told him, using the words as a form of surrender.

'And why not?' he demanded, the triumph gleaming in his eyes telling her that he knew he had won, whatever she might say to the contrary.

'Because you've not grovelled enough,' she informed him. 'I want you at my feet, Mac,' she warned. 'As far as I am concerned, nothing less than your complete subjugation will make up for what you've been putting me through.'

'Then get in the car,' he coaxed. 'Let me drive us home so I can subjugate myself to your heart's content.'

'Home—where?' she demanded, remembering even if he didn't that he had at least three different places he called home.

'Chelsea, of course,' he replied. 'It's too damned far for us to go to Berkshire—especially the way I'm feeling right now,' he added wickedly.

'And what about the Knightsbridge place?' she reminded him. 'Do I still not warrant entrance into there?'

'Blow the Knightsbridge place,' he dismissed, bundling her into the car. 'I haven't been near it since you walked out of Chelsea!' he told her, once he'd climbed in beside her. 'The only bed I want to sleep in, my darling bunny rabbit,' he murmured huskily, 'is the one I share with you. And that is where we are going right now!'

'Is this low enough for you?' he murmured later as she lay supine on their bed, groaning at the exquisite pleasure his tongue wreaked against the sole of her foot.

'No. I want more,' she demanded greedily.

'More?' He threaded moist kisses across her toes, then the arch of her foot, then her slender ankle. 'This kind of more?' he requested dutifully.

'Mmm,' she sighed. 'More of more.'

'Heartless woman,' he mocked, and slid himself upwards until he was lying beside her. 'Say you'll marry me and I'll give you a whole lot more,' he coaxed.

'Name the more,' she insisted non-committally.

He was quiet for a moment, his tongue playing absently with the silken lobe of her ear. Then he said quietly, 'The love kind of more, the marriage kind of more, to a man who loves you, and——' he levered himself up to look deeply into her eyes '—the children kind of more.'

'Children?' She looked searchingly into his eyes. 'You really want more children?'

'More little Lulus running rings around me?' he pondered, then smiled. 'Of course I want more children,' he assured her. 'Your children—our children—beautiful little people with beautiful minds and a wicked stepsister to keep them in line.'

'Lulu isn't wicked,' Roberta protested. 'She's just—protective of those she loves, that's all.'

'You're only saying that because she suddenly became protective of you,' he derided. 'Well?' he then asked. 'Are those enough mores, or have I got to waste time racking my brains for *more* mores?'

Roberta pretended to think about it, her fingers playing with the fine black hair at his temple, while he watched her with the growing fire of passion burning through the love in his eyes. Then, 'OK,' she surrendered, 'I'll take what you're offering, so long as you pass this last test.'

'And what's that?' he asked, smilingly taking the bait.

For an answer she pulled his naked body on top of her own, then wound her long legs tightly around him.

'More,' she whispered, and watched with a thrill as his eyes spiralled into dark clouds of stormy passion and he thrust himself deep inside her.

And he filled her—just as he had always done. Filled her with his body, with his passion, and now with the power of his love.